THE ART OF
LOVE and LIES

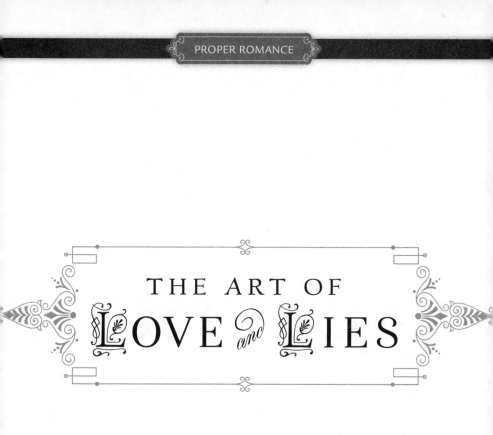

THE ART OF
LOVE and LIES

Rebecca Anderson

SHADOW
MOUNTAIN
PUBLISHING

Library of Congress Cataloging-in-Publication Data
Names: Anderson, Rebecca, 1973– author.
Title: The art of love and lies / Rebecca Anderson.
Other titles: Proper romance.
Description: [Salt Lake City]: Shadow Mountain, [2023] | Series: Proper romance | Summary: "Artist Rosanna Hawkins and Detective Martin Harrison are just beginning their romance when a priceless Michelangelo is stolen from the Art Exhibition in Manchester—and all signs point to Rosanna as the thief. She must find the real thief and return the stolen painting before she loses her chance at love—and her freedom"—Provided by publisher.
Identifiers: LCCN 2023001270 | ISBN 9781639931088 (trade paperback)
Subjects: LCSH: Artists—Fiction. | Art thefts—Fiction. | Eighteen fifties, setting. | Manchester (England), setting. | BISAC: FICTION / Romance / Historical / Victorian | FICTION / Romance / Clean & Wholesome | LCGFT: Romance fiction. | Historical fiction. | Detective and mystery fiction.
Classification: LCC PS3623. I545 A84 2023 | DDC 813/.6—dc23/eng/20230228
LC record available at https://lccn.loc.gov/2023001270

Printed in the United States of America
Publishers Printing

10   9   8   7   6   5   4   3   2   1

FOR MY MOM,
who taught me to love art

CHAPTER 1

Manchester, June 1857

ROSANNA HAWKINS could not see the dab of paint on her nose, but she could feel it. Her skin puckered in the way it always did beneath drying oil paint. Determined to finish the last touches of the piece before Anton arrived, she gave the tip of her nose a quick scratch with the end of her brush and dabbed in a few final strokes of color in the storm cloud.

This painting, her latest reproduction of a Thomas Cole landscape, was expected for delivery by tomorrow, and Mrs. Ellsworth always paid extra for promptness, which Anton passed along to Rosanna.

Mrs. Ellsworth preferred to do her business with Anton Greystone, which Rosanna found a bit silly since she'd known the woman for years. The Ellsworths lived near Rosanna's own parents in Cheetham Hill, the area of Manchester containing the stateliest manor homes. Mrs. Ellsworth's newest hobby was showing the neighbors how many paintings she could collect and display in her home. It was no matter to Mrs. Ellsworth that the paintings were reproductions; many wealthy families filled in their art collections with replicas of famous works.

Rosanna's own parents had a small assortment of good paintings, but she had never offered them one of her repro-ductions. In fact, they knew very little about her daily work. Rosanna and her sisters, Lottie and Ella, had been given the privilege of governesses and masters to help them hone their talents, and the further privilege to seek employment doing the work they loved. As their parents told them, there were many facets to growing up and finding their places in the world, and one of those facets was finding fulfilling employ-ment.

Rosanna and her sisters appreciated their parents' ex-pansive modern views, but not every family agreed that the Hawkins girls' forays into public life and employment were admirable. So many families held to the outmoded idea that young women reached the height of their worth and useful-ness by being sufficiently decorative and ensnaring wealthy husbands. Employment was not only unnecessary but rather vulgar in their minds. Mrs. Ellsworth might have looked down her nose at Rosanna's chosen work, but she had no complaints about the products she purchased.

"They want their nice little paintings, and they want them quick," Anton said.

Rosanna chose not to respond to the idea that her can-vases were "nice" and "little." She knew her paintings were masterful. Indeed, they were indistinguishable from the orig-inals. Let him say what he would; Anton was a businessman, not an artist, after all.

Rosanna's artistic talent could match any style, be it

modern, like Cole, or classical. Her Renaissance work was in high demand among their clientele, the wealthy who either loved art or wished to be seen as understanding it.

Not only did Rosanna's work reflect each stroke, each layer, and each detail of the masterworks she reproduced, she did it all with a speed that astonished and delighted her employer, Anton Greystone.

"The formulation of the piece takes far more time than the execution," she'd told Anton when he complimented her swiftness of production. She was not being modest. She understood that what she was doing was far more craft and less art. She was not a creator.

She was a professional imitator, for better or for worse.

Anton had used the word "copyist," but she objected strongly to the negative connotation of that word. She didn't copy. She *reproduced*. Simply, clearly, and with a great deal of skill, Rosanna made what she referred to as "parlor versions" of masterworks to sell to the emerging upper-middle class of Manchester, as well as to some of the higher classes who preferred their paintings less expensive.

Anton promised that as his connections continued to expand, so would her client base, and that before long, her reproductions would fill not only local houses but also the drawing rooms and parlors of fine homes from London to Glasgow and beyond.

"Your work will be everywhere," he liked to say.

She would nod in assent, all the while knowing that her invisible signature on each piece would never be seen by others, never be connected to her, never bring her fame.

And who, she asked herself, needed fame? The joy of a

finished piece was her reward. That, and a healthy percentage of the sale price.

Rosanna stepped back from her easel and examined the reproduction before her from each angle. She had studied the original in minute detail and could recall every feature.

She smiled at the canvas, pleased with the result. This was her first completed Cole; the American's work was underappreciated by Anton's clients in Manchester, who preferred paintings from artists with Italian names. Very well, Rosanna knew. She could have been a student in the school of Raphael or Michelangelo for how naturally those masters' styles came to her.

If, that was, she had been Italian. Hundreds of years before. And a man.

Not worth regretting, of course. Rosanna delighted in the privileges of living in the modern era with Victoria on the throne and opportunity for all.

Rosanna replaced her brush and removed the vial of clear varnish from her case. It was not a common addition for most artists, but Rosanna had noted that several Dutch artists had been adding the finish to their works over the past decades. Varnishing an entire painting could keep it free from dust and filth while preserving the shine of just-applied color. But Rosanna used only a tiny amount, adding a minuscule spot of varnish to the lower left corner of each of her reproductions.

It was not precisely a signature, but it was her own mark. Under ordinary household lighting, no one would ever know the mark was present, but Rosanna felt a rush of pride in knowing how to quickly distinguish her reproductions from the originals they so perfectly reflected.

At the sound of a knock, she screwed the top onto the vial, tucked the varnish away, and pulled at the apron covering her day dress, straightening out the inevitable wrinkles.

Opening the door of her suite of rooms in Mrs. Whitmore's boardinghouse, she smiled at Anton. With his dark hair, piercing brown eyes, and plaid waistcoat, Anton always looked the height of fashion, which he said was not a function of vanity but rather a necessity of business.

"Clients," he often said, "need to see they are working with a serious man."

Seriousness, Rosanna was certain, was not the first thing their patrons noticed. Anton's smooth, charismatic polish and his intensity of address made the middle-aged women of Manchester swoon beneath the gaze of his dark-browed eyes, but the handsome suit did not hurt, and altogether the method worked for him.

He leaned forward and brushed her cheek with a peremptory kiss. She tried not to be bothered by the bristles of his beard and moustache any more than by his expectation that such kisses were always welcome. The line between their business relationship and their personal one had become blurred, which Rosanna recognized was mostly her fault, as she had little energy for stating and restating boundaries.

She led him inside the room to where her easels stood near a large window.

"How is the American coming?" he asked, removing his hat and tossing it on a small table near the door.

"Just finished," Rosanna said.

"Already? That's my speedy bunny," he said, chucking her beneath her chin in a way that she tried to find endearing.

His propensity to call her silly pet names and bestow occasional kisses on her cheek was part of his carefully curated business image. She didn't mind, really, and she knew she ought to feel grateful: he was universally seen as handsome, he employed her in a manner that she loved, and he fed her a steady stream of compliments—even if those compliments occasionally struck her as insincere or unflattering.

Perhaps someday she would meet a man who wished to know the workings of her mind, not only of her paintbrushes. A man who spoke her name with an accent of wonder.

Anton stalked around the drying painting, his long legs lifting as though in a march as he tilted his head this way and that, checking it from the sides, the top, and, with a creaky bend of the knees, from beneath. His motion reminded her of an overgrown spider on hinged legs.

At length, he nodded. "You have done it again. Just as expected."

Rosanna lowered her eyes, wishing for a moment that her work would strike him as more than merely expected. She remembered when his eyes used to fill with delight, when he used to consider her work the stuff of genius, or at least brilliance.

Over the course of their business arrangement, that initial delight had morphed into inevitability.

But she knew she was in an extremely desirable situation, so she chose not to complain.

"What a grand team we are," he said, standing behind her and wrapping his arms around her as they both looked at the Cole reproduction. He spoke with his mouth near her ear, warming her. "You, making these pretty paintings so the working-class wealthy can festoon their walls and halls with pictures. Me, bowing and smiling and willingly taking their money."

"I suppose I could bow and smile and take money as well," Rosanna said, leaning back into Anton's vest.

He laughed. "I quite doubt it," he said. "Nobody wants to do business with a pretty little girl." Giving her a quick squeeze, he released her and spun her round to face him. "Nobody but me, that is. Because I do so love working with my bunny."

He leaned in to kiss her, but quickly drew back with a look of, if not disgust, at least concern, in his eyes.

"You've a bit of paint upon your face," he said, gesturing at her nose while wrinkling his own, as though she'd sprouted a hairy wart.

He gestured toward the closed door of her bedroom, where she kept a washbasin and a small mirror. "Do take care of that, Bunny," he said.

Removing herself to her room, she glanced at her reflection. It was only paint, she thought. Hardly worth such a reaction.

But Anton was always perfectly neat and attractive, his beard full and black, as much a badge of honor as though he'd been one of the soldiers forced to grow one by the cold of the last few winters in the Crimean.

When clients remarked on his "soldier's beard," he certainly never corrected them. It had become something of a jest to him, the way society ladies and gentlemen assumed he earned this badge of honor as had other men. He laughed as he told Rosanna of their clients' misapprehensions, as though the Manchester wealthy were so easily fooled by a trick as paltry as facial hair. They did not need to know he had not served in the army.

"Helps the deal slip along," he said with a wink at Rosanna.

She washed her face until she could see no remaining blue pigment on her skin. She lifted a nightdress from the corner of her bed and hung it on the peg behind her bedroom door before returning to Anton.

Her open smile did not rekindle his interest in bestowing a kiss, however. He stood at the easel, hands clasped behind his back, studying her work.

"This really is quite good," he said.

The compliment sent a shiver of pleasure down her arms.

"I'm so glad you think so," she said.

"Of course, I do," he replied, not turning to look at her.

She smiled at the attention even so.

He nodded again at the Cole reproduction. "It's the fastest turnaround you've done yet. If we can get more people interested in the American, we can make far more money with this kind of speed. The Italians are popular, but they take you so much longer, they're hardly worth the effort."

Rosanna's shoulders stiffened at his words. Hardly worth the effort? Which effort? Hers? Or his—the difficulty of waiting for her to finish a visually perfect and flawless reproduction of one of the greatest masterworks of all European history?

Annoyance pricked at her but did not have time to grow to anger. He requested a look at her attempts at etching.

She ought to be grateful for the change in topic, but the etchings had given her a surprising amount of trouble.

She sighed quietly and pulled a stack of the metal plates from the drawer in which she kept them. Each plate was covered with a coating of wax and tar, and then, using a series of smaller and smaller styluses, she scratched away the covering until the metal showed through in an impression of pen or pencil lines. After the etching was completed, she would clear away the waxy coating. Then she could press the plate, now covered with ink, onto a sheet of paper to transfer the image, complete and backward, onto the paper.

The work was excruciating, tedious, and vexing. Each image Rosanna tried to reproduce had issues with angles, lines, and curves. She simply could not reverse the image in her mind in a manner that could perfectly match the prints once they were pressed. Her ease in mimicking a painting did not seem to translate to etchings.

Her frustration only grew as she watched Anton's expression. She ought to be doing better. He expected her to. She expected nothing less. But the results eluded her.

Anton looked over her plates and the finished prints with a disappointed shake of his head. "These are simply not good enough," he said dismissively.

"I know that," she snapped.

Anton looked at her with raised eyebrows. "And what are you doing to improve?" he asked, his voice low and his cadence measured.

She felt anger rising. "I study the prints daily at the exhibition. I sketch them on-site, then I return here to attempt to recreate them. Something is always amiss."

"Clearly." His quick response cut her deeply.

Her skin burned from the heat within her. How dare he speak so curtly about this, her only failure?

She opened her mouth to speak in her own defense, but he turned away, shaking his head.

"Perhaps you would do better with the landscapes," he offered, shuffling through the plates as though another review of them might yield superior results.

"I have tried the landscapes, Anton," she said, struggling to keep her voice even. "Whether it be a nose or a tree, the reversing of the angle is difficult. I believe that an original etching will always suit better than the attempt at a reproduction."

His instantaneous snort filled the room. How could a sound so near a sigh hold such contempt? She closed her eyes to keep her resentment contained.

Anton shook his head. He spoke with thinly veiled annoyance, his voice pinched and reedy. "Will suit better? Suit whom, Bunny? You? Or our customers? None of whom, I need remind you, are interested in owning an original print by Rosanna Hawkins, but all of whom are delighted by the Art Treasures Exhibition's display of Rembrandt etchings."

"I did not mean to suggest—" she began, but he spoke over her.

"While that dries," he said, gesturing dismissively to the Cole reproduction, "get over to the exhibition. Draw. Study. Sketch. Stay all day if you must but make this happen." He shook the stack of etching plates at her.

When she did not respond, he shook his head and gave an aggrieved sigh. "Nothing will sell as quickly as prints of

Rembrandt etchings. Once you get this correct, it will be as simple as inking one after another after another." His words sped up, and he began to smile. "Everyone will be able to afford it, even those who would never manage to pay our price for a painting."

She wondered what that price was. Anton was disinclined to give her that information, even when she asked directly. She reminded herself that it didn't matter. She was making a very good wage. She glanced up at his face.

His eyes shone with delight, and she felt the returning thrill of pleasing him, even if she had an inkling that his happiness was tied directly to easy money. She was grateful for his approbation, and nothing added to her happiness like the idea of adding to someone else's.

She would discover the trick of making her eyes and her mind see in reverse. It couldn't be so difficult, she was certain. Her learning to see the converse image of one of Rembrandt's etchings would bring Anton satisfaction, make Rosanna's work simpler, and create beautiful art for so many of their clients.

Glad of his better mood, and all too aware of how quickly it could change, Rosanna nodded. "I shall spend the day among the prints," she said. "Perhaps today something will improve."

Anton shook his head and tilted his face down toward her. "You should know better than that, Bunny." Eyebrows lowered, he shook a finger softly in her direction. "Things don't improve. People do."

Nodding as if to agree with his own pronouncement, he said, "If you choose to work hard, the improvement will follow." He softened the blow of his words by enfolding her in his arms and pressing a kiss atop her head.

"Right. Go on, then," he said, as though dismissing her from her own rooms.

She tried not to feel a sense of relief when he stepped away and, picking up his hat, showed himself out.

MANCHESTER
HERALD-TRIBUNE

June 1, 1857

Art Treasures Drawing Crowds

Lottie Hawkins

Nearly a month into the Art Treasures Exhibition and the streets of Manchester are crowding with visitors. Locals and tourists alike throng the halls of the glass and steel structure, crowding in to witness the largest collection of artworks ever gathered in England.

If the entrance fee of half a crown kept some of our less-affluent neighbors away in the first weeks, the reduction of ticket price to a shilling has opened the doors to many more visitors.

Where else can one absorb such a vast array of world-famous art? Paintings and sculptures from private collections fill the galleries, although we might not see *all* the best art that England has to offer. A source claims that, upon invitation to display some of his private collection, one of our illustrious Dukes wonders what we might want of art here in Manchester, and that we ought to keep to our mills.

Perhaps he would do well to take a train excursion into our city to see how seamlessly we display beauty as well as create the comforts that improve British life around the globe.

CHAPTER 2

MARTIN HARRISON strode the long gallery hallways of the Art Treasures Exhibition in Manchester. The temporary building was not the only change he'd seen in the city since his return.

Many of the mills he'd known in his childhood had been replaced by slate-roofed brick-and-stone monuments to industry, while several of the older ones seemed to squat at the canals, waiting to sink into the water. More people bustled along the main roads, more carriages, more horses, and more noise. None of it, however, compared to the crowded streets of London.

After the arrest and imprisonment of his father, Martin and his mother had fled Manchester and found solace in the busyness of the city—in London, so many strangers crossed paths that no one need know their names. In the following years, Martin trained for his career and worked at many small jobs to support his mother. He was grateful that she'd seen him elevated to the office of detective before she passed away. Now, he gave all his time to his work.

And this summer, his work had brought him home—no, *back*—to Manchester.

The Art Treasures Exhibition followed on the tails of the Great Exhibition in London seven years earlier with its crystalline walls and windows and its festive atmosphere. London had dolled itself up for the Crystal Palace and the Great Exhibition, and Manchester followed on the heels of that success.

But rather than an all-purpose display of every imaginable marvel of industry, Manchester's exhibition focused on art. Mainly painting, but also drawing and sculpture, even furniture and textiles, from famous artists to local amateurs. Artworks through the ages, all on display for a daily pass or a season ticket to each and all who cared to better themselves through the absorption of art.

He had been here for several weeks as head of exhibition security, a job that thrilled him. The exhibition hall itself resided upon three acres of space in a parkland. Since opening nearly a month ago, it had seen thousands of visitors, more every day, walking through, staring at masterpieces and middling artworks, and likely finding little difference between the two.

But everyone in Manchester, not to mention visitors from London, the Continent, and as far away as America, vied for position in front of the jewel of the exhibition: Michelangelo's recently discovered fragment of a study for a Mary-and-Jesus painting, already known widely as *The Manchester Madonna*.

Martin, an expert in detection and policing, had no foolish notions about being an expert in art. In fact, the half-drawn, half-painted scrap of board drew his attention more often than other paintings on display simply because he could see no reason to consider it a masterpiece. He continued to stare at the painting when the exhibition hall was closed to the public, wondering if the majesty of the picture would somehow distill upon him.

It had not happened yet. Mary's expression continued to strike him as discouraged. And the second little boy—John, he supposed—looked distinctly petulant, possibly leaning toward sneaky. Was he pinching the little Jesus?

The other people in the painting were probably angels, he assumed, but the feathers upon the farthest one's shoulders looked more like fish scales.

Alas, for all his talents, Martin knew he was no highbrow appreciator of the finest art. But it amused him to think that the great Michelangelo may have also taken a long look at this partially completed piece and decided it was best left unfinished. Martin smirked, imagining how the artist would react to seeing this fragment of painting enthroned here, on display for the edification of all northern England.

"Not my best work, mates," he imagined the great man saying. "Take a look at something else. *Anything* else."

Martin stepped away from the Michelangelo with a nod toward the piece, as though bidding it farewell. Surely he would see hundreds if not thousands of works as he performed his duties—paintings whose worth was without dispute.

Martin's security detail, made up of several local Peelers as well as some traveling specialists from previous exhibitions in Dublin and London, were likewise uneducated in the finer points of art appreciation. But they knew how to keep order in an enclosed space. Each man on the job had, so far, met and exceeded Martin's expectations for keeping the exhibition running smoothly.

In his own experience as a junior member of security details in both London and Dublin, he learned how to scan a crowded exhibit hall for disruptions, locate the center of a disturbance rather than the louder, more visible reactors to it, and trail a suspicious character without being noticed.

Such skills had helped him rise to the position he now held, and he used each of the proficiencies every day. Mostly, he was responsible for glorified crowd control: keeping people from approaching paintings too closely, preventing children from touching the artwork, preventing their parents from loudly reprimanding them.

It was routine work, with a few exciting exceptions, such as Prince Albert's visit last month when he had come to open the exhibition. Martin managed to behave appropriately, even though he found himself dangerously close to laughing like a delighted schoolboy when the queen's husband returned his bow.

In Manchester, Martin's daily interactions with his team were kept mainly to short reports at the beginning and ending of each day, polite nods as each security officer met the others, and occasional midday passing of information—the busiest days always held the possibility of something being touched or even approached too closely. The owners of these paintings were particular about the conditions under which the artwork could be viewed.

The organizing committee had gone to great lengths to install calico coverings that could be drawn over the building's glass ceilings to diffuse the sunlight. Martin chuckled—the lengths and expense to which English people would go to dodge the few days of summer sun. He understood the need to protect the paintings, of course, but he also noted the irony of watermen standing upon the roof on dry days, pouring buckets of cold water over the glass to keep the building's interior cool as the afternoons warmed.

An officer caught his eye and nodded. Martin walked over to him. "Afternoon, Tanner. All well?"

Constable Tanner, a young recruit with more charm than police experience, grinned. "Perfectly well, sir." He seemed to hesitate.

"Go on," encouraged Martin.

Tanner scratched the side of his head and cleared his throat. "Bit of a stir at the sculptures. A vicar is standing before one of the statues, recommending that ladies protect their virtue by averting their eyes, sir."

The men looked at each other and tried to maintain professional dignity. It did not last for long.

Martin's smile matched Constable Tanner's in sincerity if not in measurable width. Martin had never met anyone who smiled as readily as this young man did.

Nodding, Martin said, "We do seem to be walking a tight line here. People have come for an education, after all. Who are we to say what they ought to learn?"

"Indeed." Tanner laughed and touched his cap as he walked away to continue his rounds.

Walking off in search of an interesting story of his own, Martin smiled at the way a gathering surely highlighted people being people.

MANCHESTER HERALD-TRIBUNE

June 3, 1857

Picture This: Classics and Modern Beauties Side by Side

Lottie Hawkins

Many of the names of painters whose works are being exhibited this summer will be familiar to the educated. European masters are on display in every corner of the Manchester Art Treasures Exhibition. Whether you seek a peek at a Rembrandt, a Reubens, or a Raphæl, you will have a grand spectacle open to your view.

In addition, a modern movement toward historicism is on display: a group of English painters calling themselves "Pre-Raphælites" explores a return to the art of fifteenth-century Italy, complete with highly realistic religious paintings as well as convincing reproductions of nature scenes.

That is not to suggest that everything on display in the Art Treasures Exhibition is a treasure. This journalist has repeatedly studied the collections of miniatures, which are as unimpressive as they are unimaginative. Such a collection would surely fit the parlor tables of many a kind, elderly British auntie.

However, each piece finds value, be that what it may, under the gaze of an attentive viewer. Come one, come all, and witness the grand collection. There is something to appeal to every taste.

CHAPTER 3

IN A CROWDED GALLERY, Rosanna stood in front of a Gainsborough, sketchbook in hand and pencils tucked in various places about her person: one behind an ear, two up a sleeve, several stabbed indiscriminately into her pinned-up hair. She turned a page and removed the pencil from her teeth, sketching the line of the background in the piece before her. The curve of the line of trees contrasted with the curves of the woman in the foreground, creating a harmonious balance that she'd trained herself to notice and reproduce.

Having observed several other people drawing and painting in the hall, she wondered how such an exhibition might have affected her own education. If a display of art such as this had been available when she was a student, would she have been given a daily opportunity to study, ponder, and experiment with copying the masters up close and in person?

The amateur artists were, she knew, the minority in attendance. Most of the audience were not sketching, but rather simply looking.

She wondered if the other patrons of the exhibition

analyzed the work the way she did. She rather doubted it, for in her experience, when it came to art, most people believed a masterpiece was masterful because someone told them it was. Something looked nice; something looked pretty. This or that painting felt familiar, and therefore was "good."

Few took time to wonder why a painting appealed to them, and fewer still could put such ideas into words, but it was a fascinating study to her. She could ask herself questions for hours as she gave her focused attention to each piece.

She moved back to study the painting at a distance, taking in the Gainsborough in its entirety, committing each line, each ray of light, each transition of color to memory. She memorized the depth of darkness in the background trees in contrast to the figure in the foreground, dressed in a frothy gown of pinks and whites.

As patrons strolled between her and the painting, she closed her eyes and saw the image in her mind.

Whenever there were few people near, specifically no security guards, she bent so close to the painting that her nose nearly touched it, memorizing brushstrokes, storing each texture in her mind.

She was confident she could replicate it flawlessly.

When, as a child, she had surpassed the painting and drawing skill of her governess, her parents had allowed her to meet with a painting master, a forward-thinking man who broke with the tradition of instructing only boys.

Mr. Benton had fine skill and a fairly wide throw, being accomplished in drawing, painting, oils, watercolor, charcoal, and crayon. With each new medium, Rosanna's skill quickly rivaled his own.

The other young girls in the group made mediocre imitations of flowers on plates, indifferent duplicates of landscapes, bland replicas of decorated vases.

Tired of mimicry, Rosanna soon began to create works of her own devising.

She began by studying a subject, watching how the light moved around a flower or how a bird in flight landed upon a branch. She lay beneath a tree and watched how the wind ruffled each leaf, causing their color to shift from deep green to silver to white and back. After her head filled with such impressions, she gathered her oils or her watercolors and played with images of light, experimenting with creating a mood.

She felt the urge to capture not precisely what she could see, but rather an indication of the feeling that came over her when sunlight glinted off a new green leaf, caught in a dew-filled spiderweb, or grew bright behind a window covering.

The small drawing room in her parents' home began to fill with her studies of color and highlight. Meanwhile, at Mr. Benton's studio, he nodded at her work and placed yet another print of an old painting before her, directing her to duplicate the strokes, the textures, and the lines.

"Sir, I should rather paint things from my own imagination," she finally admitted, sliding an original watercolor in front of him.

His reaction, a wrinkling of brow and nose, showed his distaste. "I should hope you've learned better than this," he said, a grimace furrowing a line in his forehead. "Where did you find such a piece of worthless wallpaper to copy?" He slid the paper back toward her with the tips of his fingers, lest the painting leave a mark upon him.

Rosanna swallowed down the humiliation she felt rising. She knew Mr. Benton was a great teacher, but she also knew she had made something lovely, something interesting.

"I created it," she said.

He huffed.

"It is my own idea, and my own construction." She stiffened her spine. "It is my own art."

His response was a half-laugh, half-scoff. "Art? This is no such thing. Miss Hawkins, do not misunderstand me. You are a person of fine artistic skill. You have a decent eye and a careful hand. This"—he sniffed and pointed his chin toward her painting—"is a muddy mess."

Rosanna instinctively tucked the paper beneath her table-top easel to protect it from his invective.

"I would advise you to continue to hone your talent at recreating fine art in the style that people appreciate. There is no room for a young lady to dabble in such nonsense as that." He waved his hand dismissively at the scrap of paper still showing beneath the easel.

And now, years later, Rosanna was confident she had taken Mr. Benton's best advice to heart. She had learned, much to her own artistic and financial advantage, how to recreate the art people loved. Comfortable art.

Her natural and practiced skills for replication meant Anton was able to sell her parlor reproductions as quickly and as often as she was able to produce them. She was an expert, a professional painter.

The thought made her smile.

And if the wish to create something new, something special that had never been seen before, occasionally crept into her heart, she had learned to dismiss such silliness.

Rosanna closed her eyes and recalled a small portion of the Gainsborough before turning around. She opened her eyes and quickly drew in her sketchbook. When she turned back to check her work, it was flawless.

Exactly as expected.

With the confidence born of success, Rosanna moved to the display filled with Rembrandt's etchings. Here was the next skill she needed to master.

Anton was correct, of course.

Once she mastered the etchings, they could create piece after piece with no more effort on her part than dabbing on the ink and rolling the plate onto paper. Now more than ever, the wealthy patrons of Manchester craved the kind of art on display at the exhibition. Everyone would want a tiny print of one of these marvelous etchings.

She stood before a wall filled with yellowing, framed prints, the scope of which was, by any standard, fantastic.

Rembrandt's paintings, drawings, and especially these miniature etchings, most of which would fit in the palm of her hand, were breathtaking. The detail Rembrandt managed to convey in wax and metal was stunning, and the portraits, sketched and hatched in tiny lines, practically came to life on paper. Unlike in an oil painting, each hair looked like an actual hair. She shook her head in wonder, as she did every time she came here to attempt an imitation.

But imitation was all she was able to create.

And poor and imperfect imitation, no less.

Her inability to reproduce these masterworks was a constant source of frustration. Why was the rotation so difficult? She had mastered far more difficult materials.

She stepped close to one of the simpler landscapes, taking in each line that represented a scratch into the wax covering a metal plate.

As she stared at the print, she imagined herself scraping these tiny lines, one here and there for a light segment of the picture, many crosshatched strokes together for the darkest shadows.

Rosanna turned to a fresh page in her sketchbook and drew the image before her. She placed every line, every angle on the paper. When she finished, she had perfectly recreated Rembrandt's tiny masterpiece.

How, though, to reverse the image? She had tried a mirror, to ill effect. And when she had held her paper up to the window to trace the reverse image on the back, the final product somehow looked false.

Perhaps Anton would be just as happy if she created the picture in ink on paper, just as she had with pencil. Would their buyers find any true objection to the manner in which the piece was created? She thought not. Only the finished product really mattered.

She stepped close to the portrait on her right: a man's head ringed in curls, his face open and cheerful in a smile. As she reproduced the lines, switching out her pencil as it dulled for another stuck in the twist in the back of her hair, she felt herself transported. She felt as though she could see the actual man Rembrandt had drawn, his grin palpable.

She found herself grinning back.

Fingers flying across her paper, she felt herself rocking back and forth, not quite moving her feet, but swaying to the rhythm of her heartbeat. Swift strokes of pencil on paper, eyes locked into the printed gaze of the curly-haired man, Rosanna knew that this was what it was to feel joy in her work.

Immediately after her thought, she felt an entirely different sensation.

A shoulder collided with her own, knocking pencil and book from her hands. Several other pencils flew from the knot in her hair, clattering onto the floor in a noisy rattle.

"Oh, dear. I am terribly sorry," a voice said.

Rosanna turned to see the man who spoke.

He stood, hands outstretched, as though perhaps something else would fall and he might catch it. Brows knitted together, he was all concern.

Rosanna registered the regret in his face at the same moment she noticed the line of his brow, the angle of his chin, and the set of his dark eyes.

He looked like a Renaissance hero, all symmetry and masculine beauty. His eyes were the deepest brown, nearly black, in contrast to his fair hair.

She had the foolish inclination to ask him to sit for a portrait. Immediately.

As his arms remained stretched out toward her, she wondered what his reaction might be if she simply walked into those arms.

Of course, she would never be so forward. Even if he was standing there, holding his arms mere inches from her own.

"Are you well, miss?"

"Am I well?" she repeated, unsure of his meaning. Did he intend to ask why she had not taken the step required to enter his proffered embrace?

"I'm afraid I gave you quite a knock," he said. "Please, forgive me." He appeared to notice how he was standing, as though prepared to catch her if she were to fall, and he dropped his arms to his sides, moving smoothly into a bow at the waist. The more formal attitude matched the austerity of his uniform, though she preferred it far less.

"Oh, please do not worry," she said, smiling. "You have not hurt me, sir. I simply seem to have lost control of my pencils."

He knelt on the floor, scooping up the scattered drawing pencils as well as her sketchbook, which had fallen open, revealing her most recent work. As he lifted the book, he stared from her drawing to the etching upon the wall before him.

"Why, you're an artist," he said.

Rosanna recognized the surprise in his voice. It was a common reaction when anyone saw her work.

"I draw and paint, yes," she said, holding out her hand for her things.

"But you're so . . ." He stammered. "You're very pretty, and I mean . . ."

For an instant, she felt pity for his confusion.

"You're a . . ." He did not seem to know how to complete that thought.

"I am a woman, yes. And I can paint and draw pictures."

Why was it that the public's image of a person of creative means somehow led directly to visions of a shambling, hunched, and nearsighted elderly man?

She stepped closer to where he stood, taking the pencils from his right hand. He held her sketchbook tightly in his left, as though he had no intention of letting it go.

She leaned closer, seeing precisely the effect that her proximity had on his growing confusion. She held back a smile.

He did not attempt to speak again, but she was unwilling to end their encounter.

"You may find," she said, her voice low and even as she reached to pull her book from his clutch, "that many women, the handsome as well as the plain, have impressive abilities of various kinds." She let her smile show.

His cheeks flushed a becoming shade of pink. Rather than make him seem flustered, his blush made him appear as though he'd been taking pleasant and vigorous exercise outdoors.

Still, he said nothing.

"I believe there is another pencil there, behind your foot," she said, pointing. "If you don't mind . . ."

He bent gracefully and retrieved it, then bowed over her hand as he placed the pencil in her palm. She had to admit, he was far more agile than their initial physical encounter would have led her to expect.

"Is there any particular reason you chose to pass this way today?" she asked him, hoping to hear his voice again. "Or is it simply my good luck that I was standing here as you barreled through?"

His face flushed a deeper red, but her smile coaxed an answering grin from him.

"I was distracted. Looking where I had been, instead of where I was going. My apologies, miss," he said, his smile adding to his attractiveness by the second. Goodness, but she wanted to draw him this moment.

He had not asked her name, but his words did give her an opportunity. "Hawkins," she said, stabbing her pencils back into the knot of hair at her neck and then proffering her hand. "Rosanna Hawkins."

He took her fingers in his large hand, and she felt warmth race up her arm.

"An honor, Miss Hawkins. I am Inspector Martin Harrison, at your service."

Inspector. How official.

"And what, Mr. Harrison, are you inspecting?" She arched her eyebrows and met his eyes. Far too bold, she knew. Alas, she did not care. A moment like this, an opportunity for some harmless flirting with a handsome stranger, came far too rarely in her life.

He laughed. "I operate the security detail here at the exhibition."

It had not truly occurred to Rosanna that this place would have an organized security operation, but of course, she realized, there was more fine art on display here in this field in Manchester than was likely in the entire Louvre Museum in Paris.

She arranged her features into an expression of serious concern. "And do you find this a difficult venue to secure? Are there dangers lurking in the galleries?" She could not keep the smile from appearing at her own jest.

"None as yet," he answered in a light tone, his smile bright even as the flush receded from his cheeks.

"In which case, I must know. How did you come to rush

into this gallery and smash into me? Were you so distracted by these remarkable etchings that you failed to see me altogether?"

"I confess, my back was turned." He made no further excuse, but his eyes did not leave hers. Was he finding it as difficult to rein in his smile as she was?

She leaned closer, lowering her voice as though to share a secret. "What if I had been hatching some nefarious plot? Would you have missed it completely?"

He shook his head, tousling his golden hair. "I should think that, in the case of plots either nefarious or benign, we were destined to bump into each other today. Fate would have demanded it."

She laughed. "Who are we mere mortals to defy fate?"

He answered with another radiant smile.

MANCHESTER HERALD-TRIBUNE

June 4, 1857

Mingling among the Masters
Lottie Hawkins

As visitors continue to swarm the Art Treasures Exhibition, witnessing Classicism, Modernism, and Romanticism, this journalist has witnessed several Romantic encounters of the human variety.

Youth will gather where they may, and it appears *they may* inside the exhibition's many galleries. Perhaps they take inspiration from Gainsborough's paintings of flirtations or Mr. Robertson's photographs of handsome soldiers serving in the Crimean.

Whether the artworks inspire the *rendezvous* or simply serve as background for them, the young and the young at heart are making free to share glances, stand close together, and steal the occasional kiss.

Perhaps on your next visit to the exhibition, you can catch a glimpse of some artful interactions that do not hang upon the walls.

CHAPTER 4

ROSANNA HAWKINS. Martin smiled at her playful comments and wished he had reason to speak her name aloud. But why had he introduced himself in such a stiff, overstuffed manner?

Inspector Martin Harrison. As though she might recognize the name that he'd inherited from his father as the shameful tag it was, as though she needed the clarification that he was the Martin who was an inspector and not the Martin who was a prisoner in Australia.

At least the old man would not make an appearance at the exhibition to surprise him, Martin thought.

"May I," he asked Miss Hawkins, "assume that you can find it in your heart to forgive me for the abrupt manner in which I made your acquaintance today?"

The lovely woman dipped her chin and looked with a sense of demure politeness down at the floor. "As you say, Inspector Martin Harrison, who are we to argue with fate?"

When she glanced back up, the sparkle in her eye and the banter in her smile struck him with a jolt equal to what he'd felt when he'd touched her hand. A playful woman of intelligence and beauty. What a delight.

He nodded, feeling unequal to the task of keeping up with her jesting, but as she stood there, watching him watching her, he knew he must respond.

"Is this your first visit to the Art Treasures Exhibition, Miss Hawkins?" he asked.

She readjusted an errant pencil in her knot of curls. "If it were, would you have secret gems to unfold to my view?"

He could not be completely certain if she teased. "Perhaps," was all he felt confident to say. He dared not over-promise, as he had little idea of how well she knew the exhibition, and he very much wanted to keep her nearby.

She gestured to the long gallery before them. "By all means," she said, "lead on, Inspector."

Martin hardly knew what possessed him, but he held his arm out to the lady. She rewarded him with a smile and her hand pressed to the inside of his elbow. She tucked her sketchbook beneath her other arm.

Dragging his eyes from her face was a trial, but he had already caused her bodily harm today, and they'd only met a few moments earlier. He must watch his step.

As they moved down the gallery, he realized she had not, in fact, told him if this was her first visit. Nor if she were local, nor if she were single.

He had referred to her as "Miss Hawkins," but she had not specified. Nor had she corrected him, which was small comfort. However, the thought that a large and angry husband might appear around any corner was enough to keep

Martin's glances short. This would be nothing but an official tour.

Not that he'd ever given an official tour before. Nor, if it came to it, had he received one.

"These are quite pretty," he said, gesturing to some landscape paintings.

"Indeed, they are," she agreed. Did she sound disappointed? "Though, there are those who consider landscape the lowest in the hierarchy of paintings."

He swallowed. How to repair this latest blunder? "Are you one of those?"

She laughed. "How delightful of you to pretend my opinion matters," she said. "And since you asked, no. I think a well-composed landscape is delicious to the eye."

You are delicious to the eye, he wanted to say. But he did not. "Your opinion matters to me," he said instead. "Between the two of us, you are the talented artist."

She shrugged, but the smile that curled the edge of her mouth led him to believe he had not muddled the whole conversation. "I am the painter," she corrected. "And you," she added, "are the tour guide."

He stopped. "Unless you should prefer to guide me?" he said, hoping beyond hope she would agree to lead their wanderings.

"I would not dare to presume," she said. But again, there was a flash of humor about her mouth. That lovely mouth.

He pointed to a collection of paintings that all had a similar look about them. Without looking closely enough to read the label beside each frame, he guessed they were all done by the same painter.

"What do you think of this one?" he asked.

Miss Hawkins stepped close to the large painting in its ornate frame. Martin kept pace with her, so she need not drop her hand from his arm.

"It makes one wonder how painters decided to position their models," she mused. "Why, for instance, is this woman holding this piece of paper?"

"She's reading a love letter from her sweetheart," Martin replied instantly. That much was clear.

"Do you think so?" she asked. "See her expression. Does that look like the raptures of love to you?" Miss Hawkins drew her face into a passable reflection of the blank stare of the subject.

"I should only be able to guess," he said, "but I imagine perhaps their love has grown somewhat stale."

She nodded. "I agree. This is not the blush of first love. But it is more than that—she is not carried away by her passion, but not because their amour has diminished."

She leaned closer to the painting, carrying Martin with her. He made certain to halt his lean to keep them at a safe distance from the artwork.

They gazed at the detail of the picture.

"The true reason for her lack of longing is that this letter is not from her beloved at all," Miss Hawkins said.

"No?" Martin asked, a smile playing at his mouth.

"No," she said, with a sad shake of her head. "It is a missive from her steward reporting the household spending. She is weary of his accounts of the price of beef and rice. It is all rather shocking, but she has grown tired of being shocked.

See how she counts on her fingers?" She pointed out three fingers raised on the woman's hand.

When she seemed to need a response, Martin said he did, indeed, see her fingers.

"She counts not the days until the return of her darling, but the weeks until she can sack the steward and hire someone with better financial sense." Miss Hawkins retained her serious expression, but she touched her finger lightly to the side of her nose and gave Martin a barely perceptible wink.

A wink.

Had he imagined it?

He hoped not, but real or imagined, it gave him courage to carry on the jest.

"Lucky for the artist to have arrived just in time to capture this critical moment," Martin said, drawing a laugh from the lady.

"Exactly," she said. "That is precisely the luck any artist must hope for. This is, as you surely know, the reason one offers sacrifices to one's muse."

She was utterly charming.

"And this?" he said, pointing out another painting in the hopes he could keep her talking. "What about this one?"

She shook her head, her expression solemn. "I should not tell you."

"Whyever not?" Martin asked.

Miss Hawkins sighed. "I do not believe you are equipped for a disappointment of this magnitude."

He straightened. "I shall endeavor to withstand it."

She smiled again, and in her attempt to hide it, a dimple

appeared in her cheek, the sight of which made him forget what he was attempting to withstand.

She shook her head. "Well, sir, if you insist. Prepare yourself."

Martin nodded, hoping to convey his preparation.

"This child," Miss Hawkins said, gesturing to the painting, "is not the owner of this dog."

He gasped in a breath of feigned outrage. "The artist attempts to lead us astray? To rewrite history in such a scandalous manner? How dare he?"

"We cannot deny that this is a healthy young girl nor that the dog is a fine specimen. But they do not, in fact, reflect the truth of the moment."

"And what is the truth?" Martin asked, delighted by the game.

"Her real pet is a pig."

At this, Martin was taken aback. "A pig?"

She nodded. "Fine Flemish families of this period often kept pigs as pets in their manor houses."

"Sounds like a potential disaster."

"Exactly," she said. "This young lady demanded that she sit for her portrait with her pig. Her mama allowed it, but as soon as the painter had finished, the mama blotted out the pig and demanded he replace it with a spaniel."

Martin continued to play along, hoping with every sentence he would see another glimpse of her smile. "Whatever for? If the pig were a beloved pet, should it not be in the painting?"

"Beloved pet for the moment, it is true," she said, shaking her head and adopting a sad countenance. "But very soon a delicious ham. And, therefore, a tragic reminder of happier days."

He nodded along with her. "And perhaps happier meals."

She laughed. He grinned at the sound.

"So this animal is a counterfeit. It's dreadful, truly." He sighed. "If we cannot trust artists to present history in its truth, whom can we trust?"

She gave an adorable shrug of her shoulders, as if to say there could be no solution.

He was not finished with this game. "Which dog sat for the painting?"

"It hardly matters, does it?" Miss Hawkins shook her head. "The outrage continues. The damage is done. History is twisted into another of art's bitter lies."

"That seems a bit harsh," he said. He assumed she was still jesting.

"Art ought to reflect fact."

"Truth and fact are not always the same thing," Martin said.

She stopped short. "What do you mean?" The playfulness was gone from her voice.

He wondered which part of his silly repartee had offended her.

"Oh, nothing at all," he said, regretting the change in her tone.

She dropped his arm and stepped away, facing him. "No, I want to understand. What did you mean?"

He rubbed the back of his neck, far more nervous in the direct path of her gaze than he had been at her side. "Simply that there are some feelings that are true, that will always feel true, that are occasionally at odds with fact. And some facts that, although real and provable, will ever ring false."

She said nothing, simply stood and watched his face as he spoke.

His cheeks warmed uncomfortably under her stare. He wished above all things that he had kept his fool's mouth shut. How to repair this?

"It's a silly thought, really, and I should not have mentioned it." He turned to stand beside her once again. He looked away from her at the painting on the wall, but he could feel her eyes on his face.

He would not have dared stare at her so openly, and he could not decide if he envied her audacity or felt offense at her effrontery.

Why did she continue to stare so?

If she did not look away soon, he would be forced to take some grave action.

She continued to stare.

"Miss Hawkins, I cannot bear to look at this painting for one moment longer, and it is terribly awkward for me to turn and witness your wrathful gaze straight on. Do me the honor, if you will, of training your eye elsewhere for a moment."

The sound of her laugh was unexpected music.

She turned so her back was to him. "Will this do?" she asked, all the playfulness returning to her voice.

"I believe this will do very well," he said, relief washing over him as he studied the pencils stuck in the hair gathered at the nape of her neck. "I apologize for saying something foolish that changed the flavor of our discussion."

She shook her head, causing the pencils to wiggle. "Not

at all, Inspector. I have never heard anyone describe the conflict between truth and fact in quite the way I feel it. I believe your candor surprised me, if only because I heard my thoughts in your voice."

Her tone, now matter-of-fact, caused him to wonder if such an idea was unpleasant to her. For him, the thought that they shared such unlikely opinions was exciting. Endearing.

He did not know how to respond, but before he could speak, she linked her arm in his once again and said, "Will you show me the truest treasure of the exhibition?"

"The *Madonna*?" he asked.

"I can only assume we are both talking about the recently discovered Michelangelo," she said, nodding. "Likely, Madonnas abound. I cannot imagine that, even without it, this place would have any lack of religious iconography."

He smiled at her. "As you have undoubtedly deduced, I do not know much about art, but I do know my Bible stories, and I have seen near enough every familiar one illustrated here—along with plenty of religious stories I don't remember reading in my family's Bible."

Miss Hawkins nodded again, and the sly grin reappeared on her face. "Indeed, it is a well-known fact that the Italian Renaissance artists had access to a Bible that we Philistines had no need for. The illustrated version, you know. The one that showed that babies were born with mature faces, lo these many centuries. And that particularly holy people come with ready-made halos shining atop their curls. Come now, Mr. Inspector Harrison," she said, and his name in her voice sounded like a melody, "have you any real need to know what an angel looks like? How often does such a thing come up in your daily work?"

Oh, if he only dared answer her. *I know what an angel looks like,* he should like to say. *One stands before me this very moment.*

He thought the words in her direction—thought them with all his might. But, of course, he could not say any such thing, so he led her to the gallery displaying the recently discovered Michelangelo.

As they waited their turn to approach the painting, he listened to her share some of the controversial opinions of critics and historians, several of whom had denied that this piece could even be Michelangelo's work. Silently, Martin thought they were probably right.

But as Miss Hawkins laid out more and more of the current thought about the matter, Martin became convinced that not only was the painting legitimate but that, no matter how rough the piece looked, it was clearly important.

He would have believed a twig peeled from the mud on the bottom of a shoe was important if she said it was. Nonetheless, it didn't make it beautiful. Not like she was beautiful. Her eyes glittered with her delight at telling him about the painting, its discovery, and the anticipation caused by its unveiling.

And he loved watching her excitement grow.

When they reached the front of the line, she showed him the brushstrokes and structural details to support those who agreed the painting was genuine. She explained how this was clearly a piece from Michelangelo's early period, and though much of his painterly style grew far more excellent after the time, there was plenty in the subjects' expressions to defy the deniers.

Martin did little more than nod along with her.

She was far more educated in matters regarding this particular piece than he was about any art in any place in the world, but rather than make him feel ignorant for not knowing, she seemed eager to share what she had learned. And before long, he realized she had certainly been here before, standing in front of this painting and studying it.

She had been here. Had likely spent hours within these walls. They had, perhaps, crossed paths more than once. How could he have not noticed her? Surely it would be impossible to see her and not be struck by her loveliness.

She continued to instruct him, and he found her knowledge enchanting. Her passion, contagious.

Martin felt he could stand before any painting—big, small, famous, important, or trivial—in any gallery and listen to her expound. He would happily believe anything she claimed. He could spend hours. Days. Forever.

Although his opinion of the quality of the painting before him did not change, he began to at least recognize the importance of the work, its discovery, and its history.

"Inspector Harrison," a voice called out.

Martin looked over his shoulder to see one of the exhibit board members gesturing to him.

He turned to Miss Hawkins. "It appears I am needed elsewhere." He wondered if she could hear the gloom that had entered his voice at the thought of being pulled away from her. He was unsure if such understanding would be welcome. "I do hope we can continue this conversation another time, Miss Hawkins."

He reached for her hand and kissed her knuckle.

In response, she laughed. That glorious bell-like laugh. "I defy you to avoid me, sir. I am here nearly every day." Her smile underscored the challenge in her words.

A challenge he would happily accept.

CHAPTER 5

THE MORNING LIGHT crept through the window coverings in Rosanna's bedroom in Mrs. Whitmore's boardinghouse. Looking about her, Rosanna felt her daily blush of pleasure at her situation.

These rooms could not compare to the luxury of her parents' home, but after Rosanna and her parents had come to an agreement about her desire to use her talents for employment, she had found this a perfect place to live. She knew that as long as she painted for Anton she would be financially secure and able to rent rooms here in Manchester, where her own growth and change seemed to happen daily before her eyes.

Her parents had granted their permission to her independence upon the condition that she visit them in their home regularly. She and her sisters gathered in the Hawkins home every Sunday, and occasionally during the week, if it suited all parties.

Her own conditions had required that they do no such thing at her home. Her independence—indeed, her very temperament—required solitude. All family members were pleased with the arrangement. Anton came calling as often as he needed for work purposes, and occasionally her sisters would come by, but her parents let her find her space and make it her own.

Rosanna spent the day beginning the process of recreating the Gainsborough. Anton had delivered plenty of canvas, so she cut and stretched and sketched and blocked. Each line, each shaft of light matched the picture in her memory as she worked through the morning.

Stretching her arms and rotating her stiff neck, Rosanna felt her stomach rumble. She had worked without a break all the way to lunchtime.

Anton would arrive soon, so she set aside the Gainsborough and turned her attention to the finished Cole piece. She'd need to wrap it in paper for delivery. She scrutinized the nearly invisible dab of varnish in the corner: her signature.

She was under no misapprehension that she was creating anything, but she knew she was *making*. And making was a particularly satisfying activity, one which deserved, even if only for her own knowledge, her mark upon it.

She made herself a pot of tea and sat to wait for Anton. She did not need wait long.

With a knock, he arrived in a bustle of coattails and a smart new top hat, shouldering his way into her apartments.

Mrs. Whitmore, who preferred to be known as a property manager rather than a house mistress or, heaven forbid, house mother, struck a balance between the propriety of checking in all visitors to her home and glancing away as her boarders lived as they pleased. She was not the fussy matron who stood in the hallway, watching visitors with a chaperone's eye and listening at doors. Rosanna enjoyed the trust Mrs. Whitmore afforded her.

Anton stood in Rosanna's rooms with his back against the closed door, eyebrows raised. "Ready, is it?" he asked.

She sighed within herself, keeping her eyes from rolling. Would it be so difficult for Anton to begin with a pleasantry?

"It is ready. How was your day?" She wondered if she could tempt him into a bit of cheery flirting. The afternoon she'd spent in the presence of Mr. Inspector Harrison had given her a taste for such things.

"Barely begun." He flipped out his pocket watch and made a sound of disapproval. "Must hurry so I don't keep Mrs. Ellsworth waiting." He tapped the paint on the Cole reproduction. "Dry?"

"We can certainly hope so, if you are planning to go about pressing on it," she said, realizing only when she spoke that his proprietary touch annoyed her.

He merely nodded. "Very well." He took another tour of the painting, examining it from every angle. "Wrap it," he said, his careless tone sounding both bored and demanding.

"Who will frame it?" she asked as she wrapped.

"Found a new man," Anton said.

When he did not offer more, Rosanna pressed. "New in town? Or new to you?"

Anton finally turned his full attention to her. His words became more thoughtful, more careful, and his tone musical. She tried not to think it oily. "Bunny, you need not worry about these final steps in the process. Your purview is here, in your studio, where your gift resides." He stroked his beard and gave her a patronizing smile. "You keep making these pretty copies, and I'll take care of all the rest."

"I am interested in all aspects of the work," she said, hoping he could not hear the hurt in her voice. She had told him often enough that she was not a copyist. She was a replicator.

"Do not allow such worries to wrinkle your pretty little forehead," he said, leaning over to place a kiss upon the forehead in question. "Have I not always handled the business matters for my bunny?"

"You have. And have I not proven myself a valuable asset to your success?" She stood tall and straight, hoping her posture would reduce the frequency with which he used his ridiculous pet name for her.

He made a sound of dismayed expectation. "Valuable? Dearest Bunny, you are indispensable. Without you, I have nothing." He waved about his person with two empty hands, waiting until he was certain she saw the generosity of the gesture and recognized the liberality of his words. Then he moved forward and enfolded her in his arms.

As he held her, he spoke into her hair. "You make the paintings." So simple, at least to Anton. "And in turn I promise to keep you sufficiently busy and quite well paid. How many people of your prodigious talent slave away day after day, hour after hour, and sell nothing?"

He did not wait for her to answer. He did not need it. He knew that she knew, and at moments like this, she was certain he simply loved to hear the sound of his own voice.

"I have created for you a perfect opportunity. You get to paint away, wander down to the exhibition and stare at masterworks all day long, copy out other men's genius, see the effects of your labors, and build a comfortable life for yourself. Every artist's dream."

She closed her eyes and pressed down the retort that threatened to burst from her. What did Anton know of what artists dreamed? Or what Rosanna, in particular, dreamed? How could he know what should satisfy her? He had never asked.

Only assumed. Only demanded that she be pleased.

As she exhaled, she calmed a bit.

Of course, she knew she ought to be pleased. And she was pleased.

Anton was correct. This was a glorious life for a painter. But it was not quite an artist's dream.

She was not quite an artist, after all. Shaking her head, she pushed the thought away.

"Very well," she said, once she was able to produce the words with a sincere smile. She backed out of his embrace, putting a reasonable space between then. "Let us get this lovely replica into the hands of Mrs. Ellsworth so she can lord it over her neighbors."

Rosanna understood that a large portion of Anton's success came from creating a feeling of competition between his clients and their friends. A competition for which he could provide ample goods and services to all parties.

"Thus giving her neighbors reason to call upon us for their own pretty little pieces," he said with a nod.

Rosanna, very familiar with both Mrs. Ellsworth and her neighbors, did not respond. Did Anton remember, did he realize that Rosanna's own parents were among the set to whom he referred?

How odd would it be to visit their home in Cheetham Hill and find one of her paintings hanging upon the wall? Her parents purchased few paintings, all of them original.

"What have you got in the works?" Anton's mellifluous tone evaporated from his words. He was finished caressing her, both with speech and hands, and was back to business.

She gestured with her head to the Gainsborough reproduction in process.

He grunted an approving sort of noise. "How soon?"

"I believe I can manage it within a week," she said.

He looked at her with raised eyebrows. "So long?"

"A week is not very long to reproduce a masterwork," she said, sounding like a strict governess.

"Five days," he said, a challenge in his tone.

"I do not believe a negotiation on timing is at all appropriate," she said, stepping farther from him. When had he become so demanding?

"I need what I need when I need it," he snapped. "And there is something far more important coming." He checked his pocket watch again before slipping it back into his vest.

"More important?" she asked, wishing to end this conflict-laden conversation, even while knowing she must have the information. Preferably sooner than later.

"You're going to recreate *The Manchester Madonna*," he said. His smile lifted his black moustache from his beard and allowed her a glimpse of his gold incisor.

Rosanna felt the surprise of his announcement settle upon her. "The Michelangelo?" she asked, knowing full well the answer.

He picked up the wrapped Cole then nodded toward

the Gainsborough. "Finish that. Then get to work on the *Madonna*. Quickly." He lifted an envelope from his pocket and tossed it on the table. Her payment.

She had a thousand questions. Who was the Michelangelo for? How much was someone willing to pay for a reproduction of a partial work, even if it was the most important partial work on display this summer? Did she have the skill for duplicating an unfinished work? Even the least discerning eye would notice tiny differences when the piece was in such a state.

Unsure of her ability to discuss any of her concerns with Anton now, considering his shifts in mood, she said, "What of the etchings?"

He placed his hat upon his head and, turning to leave, looked at her over his shoulder. "When you figure out how to make a worthy copy, it will make us both rich. But I am not confident."

With that, he stepped out the door, and she was left alone with the blocked-in Gainsborough, a pile of unimpressive etching sketches, and the cash for the Cole.

I am not confident, he had said. And punctuated it with the closing of the door. She stared at the door, unsure whether she hoped or feared that he might return.

Anton adored her; she knew he did. But there was something unsettling about trying to maintain a business relationship with a man who bestowed kisses as often as he gave payment or orders.

And she could not help but compare the stilted, careful dance of hide-and-reveal the two of them engaged in against the delicious, warm playfulness of yesterday's conversation with Inspector Martin Harrison.

Her every comment seemed to spark Mr. Harrison's interest. He played along with her silly games, and never, in all the time they were together, did he seem patronizing or didactic. Everything he said was interesting, made increasingly so by the turn of his head, the angle of his jaw, and the light glinting in his eyes.

When had she last felt such an embrace of esteem and happiness in a conversation with Anton?

That was unfair.

She and Anton had known each other for many long months. Their relationship was the stuff of work and experience. He may not have been so attentive lately as Mr. Harrison was upon their first meeting, but how could she begrudge him that?

Relationships changed as they grew. There was little new or fresh between Rosanna and Anton. It was hardly fair to compare this first blush of flirtation with something steady.

Yet, she couldn't ignore her desire to spend the time she ought to be working on the Gainsborough walking the halls of the exhibition with her fingers tucked in the protective arm of Inspector Martin Harrison. She could easily finish the Gainsborough reproduction in only a few days, including drying time. She had built in the extra time so she might wander the galleries in hopes of reconnecting with Mr. Harrison.

She ought to be ashamed of herself.

Perhaps it was the way Anton spoke to her, his occasionally unctuous tone and his pedantic air, that made her uncomfortable rather than giddy. That was expected after knowing someone for a long while, and what could she do about it in any case? She knew better than to think she could change a person to suit her desires.

Nothing was actually amiss. Anton was not doing anything wrong. He simply did not speak to her in a manner that brought shivers of delight to her arms and blushes of pleasure to her cheeks. Ought she hold that against him?

Rosanna knew that the attractiveness of the first moments in any new friendship was strong. Perhaps Mr. Harrison, once one knew him better, would not be nearly as charming as he had seemed yesterday. How long could such playfulness really last?

How could she honestly compare the feelings of her interactions yesterday, the flushes of pleasure, with the solid assurance she felt with Anton? He saw her worth and value. He needed her. He kept her in great esteem. His work was, as he often reminded her, nothing without her.

Or someone like her. The thought came unbidden to her mind.

Was there someone like her?

Naturally. There were many like her.

Surely there were plenty of governess-trained painters, both here in the north and across Great Britain. The numbers of talented and accomplished young women in London alone must be staggering. Even here in Manchester, all the young women she knew were taught to mimic the paintings of the masters. Surely many of them could make replicas for Anton to sell.

How had such an idea never occurred to her before?

She was replaceable.

How dreadful.

Rosanna knew what she needed to do. She must make herself indispensable to Anton, and she must do it right away. She would master the etchings, even if it took her away from the pleasures of Mr. Harrison. She would reproduce a Madonna that Michelangelo himself would marvel at. She would work faster, harder, and with more skill than she ever had before, and Anton would have no choice but to admire her.

Love her artistic output.

Adore her productivity.

She would begin right away.

After she spent one more afternoon—or maybe two—in the charming and delightful company of Mr. Martin Harrison, Inspector.

MANCHESTER
HERALD-TRIBUNE

June 5, 1857

Authors Mingle with Art

Lottie Hawkins

The Art Treasures Exhibition was graced with an illustrious visitor this week. Mr. Charles Dickens, London's favorite storyteller, made his way north to wander the halls and galleries of the ATE.

He explored the galleries from the east side to the west, spending significant time inspecting several of the private collections. Perhaps he has plans to build up a gallery of his own in London Town.

This journalist was delighted to see that the famed author purchased a catalogue, several pamphlets, and a program for the musical concert by Mr. Hallé's orchestra, which performs almost every day in the special gallery built for such recitals. Such generosity of purchase allows the ATE to recoup some of its expenditures, and the exhibition staff readily expresses its gratitude to patrons who buy official merchandise at the venue.

Mr. Dickens also purchased a paper cone of spiced nuts, which he enjoyed while he walked through the gallery housing the suits of armor. Perhaps something he saw will inspire his next publication. Keep your eyes open for signs of Manchester life in Mr. Dickens's next. (May we suggest, Mr. Dickens, the thrilling tale of a newspaper journalist who, despite a dark and discouraging past, rises to previously unthinkable heights of literary merit?)

CHAPTER 6

DAY AFTER DAY, Martin found himself invited to meetings where the exhibition board sat round a large table and held conversations that did not require his experience nor his opinions. Trying not to resent these intrusions became more difficult when the meetings took him away from what had become the best parts of his days: encounters with Rosanna Hawkins.

He had found her several times over the past week. Nearly every day, in fact, which made him hope she was looking for him, as well. They had enjoyed more circuits of the galleries, and he had found himself smitten by her humor, her wit, and her loveliness. His every working day was made brighter by her company, and he could think of little else when she was not present.

Today, he steeled himself for a meeting where he knew she would not appear, but he could imagine what she would have to say about those in attendance could she invent stories for them.

When Martin entered the board's meeting room, he was

surprised to find most of the exhibition committee already present around the table. Professional organizers, many of whom had contributed to the Great Exhibition in London several years prior, had been on hand for a year before the Art Treasures Exhibition opened earlier this spring.

Along with the organizing committee were members of the upper-crust society of Manchester, men and women of means who had gathered together, rallied support, engaged families and businesses for financial donations, and overseen the formation of the buildings. These people each seemed to take not only the exhibition as a whole but also their donations in time and money terribly seriously, and any discussion of who was responsible for what rang with competing claims.

Notable among the wealthy was the Marquess of Hertford, who, Martin had learned, had loaned forty-four paintings and drawings from his home's collection to the exhibition, filling an entire corner of one gallery. Martin was not sure if that was a demand of the marquess or a concession of the committee out of a sense of duty. In either case, Martin made no attempt to chat with the marquess. It was not that he was such a fearsome gentleman, but Martin preferred to stand than to sit, and he did not have ready conversation to share.

"Ah, Inspector," said John Totten, brushing nonexistent dust from his immaculately tailored suit, "you are here, and we may begin. As head of the organizing committee, I feel it imperative to gather as many of us together as often as possible. This committee, working under my auspices, has created a wonder."

Totten waited for someone to applaud. Lady Someone of Somewhere obliged. Several others followed suit until the organizer felt he had been sufficiently honored.

"As you know, we have hundreds and hundreds of visitors each week, and our patrons run the gamut of English life." He gestured vaguely toward—Martin assumed—all of England.

"We receive, in addition to schoolchildren, mill workers, and university students, many notable guests much like yourselves." His gesture now limited itself to the room, even if it did not quite include Martin. No matter.

"And now, we will have in our very near future, the most impressive and notable visitor of all."

"Is it Mr. Disraeli?" a man of rather clear importance, if one measured such things by the height of one's top hat, asked.

Mr. Totten cleared his throat. "Ahem, no." As if to assuage any disappointment from the gathered crowd, he continued, "Although he has been sent a special invitation, and we expect to hear from him by the day." He rubbed his hands together. "Mr. Disraeli is not as impressive as the guest to whom I refer."

"Louis-Napoleon?" asked another man, one who had the hint of a French accent.

Mr. Totten glowered.

The marquess spoke at last, in a quiet voice of dignity. "Ah, Mr. Totten. Are we to be graced with another visit from His Highness, Prince Albert?"

Many of those present offered knowing smiles and

nodded, as though they had been privy to this important surprise, possibly at the lips of the prince himself.

Martin looked at Mr. Totten, who squirmed in obvious impatience. *Poor man. He should never have let them guess. He's lost control of the conversation.*

Before Mr. Totten's face turned completely red with frustration, he blurted, "Our important guest is, in fact, Her Royal Majesty, Queen Victoria."

The collective gasp seemed to bolster Mr. Totten, making him stand even straighter and taller than before. People immediately began to whisper to one another in small groups, and Totten stood above them, nodding at their conversations as though he had planned them.

Waiting to hear how his team was involved with the royal security, Martin kept his eye on Mr. Totten. Surely the man would get to the details soon.

Alas. Not soon.

Totten seemed to be lifted up and carried away by the hum of discussion around the room. He had caused a stir, and Totten was clearly a man who dearly loved to cause a stir.

After a few minutes, Martin took a step toward Mr. Totten. "Will the queen's visit require special security measures, sir?" he asked, his voice low enough not to interrupt the several conversations buzzing about the table.

"She will come with a retinue of traveling palace escorts, naturally," Mr. Totten explained, managing in those few words to cast a shadow of dubiousness on Martin's security operation. "Your work will remain as ever it is, save the need to double the number of men on staff for the hours leading up to and for the duration of the visit."

"And when will we have the pleasure of this visit?" One of the ladies seemed ready to burst from her chair with excitement. Martin wondered if she assumed that an invitation to join the queen's tour would be forthcoming. He did not doubt it. There was a great deal of money and prestige represented in this room.

"Her Majesty will be here Tuesday next," Mr. Totten said, once again gesturing to the general world about him. "And, as head of this committee, I feel it incumbent upon us to promise—and deliver—an unforgettable afternoon."

Martin suspected Queen Victoria would find the exhibition excellent regardless of the committee's actions. The halls were solidly constructed. The glazed windows in the ceilings, the finest available in England or on the Continent, allowed all available light to stream in and showcase the beauties of the collected artwork. Certainly the monarch saw many fine works of art daily, as she lived in one palace or another, but anyone who enjoyed looking at art must, by reason of volume, appreciate what had been gathered here.

He waited for Mr. Totten to deliver additional instructions, but the meeting, such as it was, seemed to break up into wagers about how Queen Victoria would arrive in Manchester, the leading assumption taking her by water to Liverpool and from there into Manchester by rail. That was, at any rate, the way the gathered gentry would choose to take the trip.

Martin caught Mr. Totten's eye and bowed himself out of

the room. The head of the committee nodded his own fare-well.

Eager to see if Miss Hawkins could be within the exhibi-tion's halls this afternoon, Martin took himself up one gallery and down the next, narrowly avoiding several collisions that could not end as auspiciously as when he bumped into Miss Hawkins on that wonderful first day.

He held the shoulder of his arm with the opposite hand, wishing he could somehow still feel the touch of her against him.

As he searched for her, he wondered how she had spent so many days here prior to their first meeting without him seeing her. For he had surely seen her every time since. Now that his eyes knew her, they could scarcely avoid falling upon her daily.

Was it possible he had passed by her as she made her earliest studies of the paintings on the walls? Was it even conceivable he could have walked by her and not seen her tumbling mahogany curls, partly held back by a quiver of pencils? Could he have seen her delicate fingers drawing lines in her sketchbook and not noticed their elegance?

Many people—men, women, and children—spent hours sketching the works on display. Could he have passed Miss Hawkins every day?

He thought not.

Something must have prevented their meeting until that week, that day which would be recorded in his memory for-ever: the way she held her head, her teasing smile, her gentle laugh that sounded like heavenly music.

Martin knew he was indulging his proclivity for the dramatic, but he could hardly help himself.

There was room for nothing in his mind but Miss Rosanna Hawkins and how long it might be until he would see her again.

If he did not see her today, ought he to find her address and arrive on her doorstep?

Could it be only days, countable days, since she had entered his life?

Martin sighed. He was being silly, and he knew it.

It was time to move forward and prepare for the visit of Queen Victoria.

After one more circuit.

Alas, he did not find Miss Hawkins. He silently cursed Mr. Totten's board meeting, which likely happened at the same time as Miss Hawkins's visit.

Having seen no sign of Miss Hawkins that day, he was no less eager to return to work the following morning. And if he tied his cravat with more care than usual, perhaps changing his shirt for a whiter version, and possibly brushing his hair forward, then back, then forward again, no one need ever know.

Martin strode the galleries and hallways searching not only for Miss Hawkins but for art pieces that she could explain to him. Each subsequent time they had met, she had amused him with another delightful story about a painting, a sculpture, or a sketch. Even when their visits together lasted only moments, he felt the same thrill of being near her and counted the minutes as the greatest moments of each day.

Stopping in front of a landscape wherein the land was the barest fraction and the sky took up much of the space, he wondered if actual clouds held as many colors as these did in the painting. He was used to thinking about clouds as white or gray. But here were clouds with tips of purple and echoes of red and even green. Was that reflective of nature? Had he never noticed clouds before? Or was this a trick of art; some kind of "truth" that was not quite "fact"? He would ask Rosanna. She would know.

Rosanna. He had known her less than a full week, seen her only a handful of times, and was already thinking of her by her Christian name.

Times were changing, he reminded himself. Rules of attraction between men and women may have been unchanging since the first epochs, but rules of courtship evolved with the times just as a person's expectations did. If she did not mind his use of her given name, he ought to feel no unease about it. Of course, he would wait to be invited to use it aloud.

Courtship. Had he really been thinking of courtship? His own brazen imaginings surprised him. He could no more assume that Miss Hawkins would accept his suit than he could sprout wings and fly to her house.

And why should she? As far as he could tell, she was an upstanding woman of unimpeachable character, from a family peopled with uprightness. She must have a mother who cared for her, a father who worked, or one who had no need of employment, brothers and sisters. Her life, as far as Martin knew, was without stain.

And then there was his plight.

As few as two generations ago, a man with a devastating family history such as his own would suffer for the misdeeds of a miscreant father for the rest of his life. But now, men and women could rise above their beginnings. People could—and did—exceed the expectations of their origins, earn money to buy property and status, and overcome the personal and social horrors of shame and scorn.

Ought he not to hope for courtship? Everything was different now.

Well, not everything. But enough was different that perhaps nothing was impossible, or at least very little seemed impossible to Martin. Perhaps she could choose him despite his family's stain.

All morning and long into the afternoon, Martin walked the corridors, gazing down each gallery in search of Miss Hawkins. He had not left the halls all day. Ignoring the grumbling of his stomach, he marched up one hallway and down the next. He allowed himself to pause at the intersections, glancing upward and checking his watch. In every other instance, his eyes were on each person visiting the exhibition.

Watching for her.

When he resumed his circuit, Martin looped around the Michelangelo display, realizing that his selfish motivations of the day had likely led to crowds growing larger at certain areas, knots of people forming before the most popular of the paintings. He had been delinquent, but he was determined to do better now.

With a shake of his head and a realignment of his shoulders, he straightened into attention. For the rest of the afternoon, he attended to each aspect of the exhibit, directing patrons this way and that, answering questions, encouraging politeness of behavior.

He didn't see any sign of Miss Rosanna Hawkins, but he felt he had made a good job of watching out for her. Tomorrow she would be that much easier to find.

His vigils met with success, for the next day had hardly begun when he made his first cursory march through the halls and stopped short.

A cascade of brown curls stabbed through with several pencils snatched his attention. She stood, her eyes locked on *The Manchester Madonna*, one hand clutching her sketchbook, the other a pencil.

As he watched, she laid in every line of each figure, finished and unfinished, in the piece. Without taking her eye off the Michelangelo, she flipped the page and began again, this time reaching without looking to pull a pigmented pencil from her hair. He watched her block in the reds of fabric, the golds of hair, the blues of drapery. In a matter of minutes, she had a passable recreation of Michelangelo's masterpiece on the page.

Flip. Another blank page, and another quick sketch. This time, a close view of the babies' heads, looking opposite directions, both with that uncanny adult look about them.

Finally, after standing motionless for several minutes watching, Martin stepped forward and spoke near her ear. "I am sorry, miss, but there are hundreds of people who have come from near and far to get a glimpse of the painting you are standing in front of. I think it's time you moved along."

He stepped in front of her. If he'd hoped to win a laugh, he was disappointed.

Rosanna's face was expressionless. She had a look of uncompromising concentration and seemed not to recognize him.

He smiled at her, inviting a repeat of the other days' attentive interactions.

Nothing. Her face blank, she did not even register him.

He touched her arm lightly. "Miss Hawkins? Are you well?"

At that, she seemed to shake herself out of her reverie.

"Inspector," she said, her voice shaking. "I did not see you there." She rubbed her eyes and forced her gaze away from the painting.

Leading her away from the group forming at the Michelangelo, he took the liberty of speaking low into her ear. "Are you well?" he asked again, not knowing how else to articulate his concern. He could hardly ask her if it was usual for her to completely lose her bearings and fall into a trance while standing and sketching a painting.

Those few seconds had wrought a change in her. She looked up at him and smiled. "I am, indeed, perfectly well. Just as I was when you asked me the same question before. You do concern yourself with my well-being. I have been working, you see, and every bit of my concentration was attuned to my sketches."

"Sketches of that?" he asked, pointing to the Michelangelo.

She gave him a grin like a gift. "You needn't sound so

surprised. I assure you, many others have sketched this painting since the exhibit opened."

He nodded. "True, but I thought you were more interested in the pretty paintings."

"The pretty paintings?" she repeated, her voice holding a hint of frost.

"I mean no disrespect to Mr. Michelangelo," he said, "but you must admit, this one is not as interesting as the ones he, well, finished."

"Firstly, Michelangelo is his given name," she said, that asperity still curling about the edges of her words. "And if my Italian were as good as it ought to be, I'd tell you his proper surname." There was the grin that melted away some of the coolness.

"Proper names or not, there are many pictures here that are nicer than that one." He hoped his banter would rekindle some of their previous playfulness.

But she was not finished. "Insofar as this piece is incomplete, you might assume that it is being given too much attention here."

"Might? It is dangerously overpraised."

She tilted her head. "To what degree of danger, I must know?"

He tried to keep an air of authority about him as he replied, "Gets rather crowded here. There is the strong possibility of jostling happening right there in front of the piece."

She looked charming when she quirked her eyebrow just so.

"Jostling aside, the painting is a very good example of Michelangelo's early work, and whether it is *pretty* or *nice* does not determine if it is important, or even good. And that does not begin to take into account our enchantment of being among the first people to see a painting so recently discovered and brought into public view." She clasped her hands in front of her. "Think how long this piece remained in a locked room somewhere, far from any appreciative eyes."

He believed he hid his lingering contempt when he said, "But it's an unfinished picture, only half made."

"Yes, but that is not the point. And"—she sent him a look of amusement—"we have discussed this before. Surely you can see how even in its unfinished state, it is masterful." She gestured toward the painting, but he saw only her elegant fingers, the tips smudged with pencil lead and stained with ink and paint.

He glanced once again from the painting to the woman at his side. "Shall you think far less of me if I confess I cannot? It is no more than half a picture to me, and the children there—the babies? They send a wicked shiver up my spine." He gave an exaggerated shudder. "Something about their faces." He lowered his voice to a whisper. "They look rather mad."

Eyes wide, Rosanna gasped. "That verges on blasphemy, Inspector." But her teasing smile erased the sharp edges of her words. She reached for his arm. "We might never agree about that painting, sir. Shall you show me something new you've discovered since we last spoke?"

He nodded, grateful that his continued lack of excitement about the painting had not offended her. He watched her as they walked, cautious for her safety. When he had

interrupted her sketching, she had looked so dazed and unaware of her surroundings that he feared she might fracture.
She had seemed so fragile, so vulnerable. But now, walking
the galleries and hallways, she was as vibrant and delightful as
she had been in their previous meetings.

He led her to a portrait of a woman, sallow of face but
with the most glorious head of curls.

"Where," Martin asked, "does an artist find a model with
so plain a face and such remarkable hair?"

"Wigmaker," she responded instantly.

"You doubt this hair belongs to this woman?" Martin
laughed. "Does that not smack of removing her only beauty?"

"Oh, I'm confident this woman has truly exceptional
feet."

Martin laughed. "How would you know?"

"There are some people who bare their beauties for all the
world to see," she said.

He wondered if she could see him blush.

"Oh, poor inspector. I simply meant that some people
have pretty faces, nice ears, etcetera. You need not cringe."

Blast. She *had* seen.

She continued, gesturing to the painting. "Now you need
not ask me how I can tell the quality of this woman's feet
when the painting does not include anything below her waist.
Here is how I know. See the look of utter unconcern on her
face? How she sits for the painter without a worry clouding
her eye or a care wrinkling her forehead? She is focused, ob-
viously enough, on the state of her feet. See how she very
clearly is not looking downward? That is because she has,

insofar as her feet are concerned, nothing for which to be ashamed."

With a nod, Miss Hawkins led him away from what he would, in the future, always consider the wigmaker's advertisement.

Martin smiled and leaned nearer to her. "Did you just pull me away from that portrait because you have no better evidence for your claim than that which you have already given?"

She turned her face up to his, grinning with an unrepentant air. "Oh, dear, have you discovered my faults so early in our friendship?" She once again placed an ink-stained finger alongside her nose, caught his eye, and winked. He loved that gesture, one that suggested a shared joke.

"I admit I find no fault in you," he said. He wished he could say more.

She made a humming sound and looked up at him, eyebrows raised in an unasked question.

He shook his head, but she was not finished.

"It is perhaps unforgivable of you to see through me so easily," she said.

The arch of her eyebrow made it difficult for Martin to pay strict attention to her words. Could she have really frightened him earlier with her distant and withdrawn expression?

"Have I offended you?" he asked, certain she was teasing.

She patted her hand against the crook of his arm. "I am distressed that you are a very respectable detective." Nothing in her tone suggested any manner of suffering, and he quickly joined in her bantering.

"Why is such a thing distressing, if I may inquire?"

She shook her pretty curls and gave a delightful pout. "I shall never be able to get any of my lies past you. And now we shall have nothing else to say to one another." She looked off to the side and breathed a great sigh. "This is indeed unfortunate."

Martin spoke through his smile. "I would be willing, in your special case, to believe at least one of every three of your lies."

"Oh, no." Rosanna shook her head and dislodged a pencil. "I require my inspectors to remain upright in their duties." She tucked the pencil back into the knot of curls. "Unless perhaps you would be willing to believe two of every three?"

"We are bargaining now?" He grinned down at her and saw her smile slip. He was not sure what he had said to make that happen, so he quickly spoke, hoping to bring back the full smile. "Very well. I accept. I shall believe, at minimum, two of every three lies you tell me."

She removed her hand from his arm and held it out to shake. "We have reached an accord, sir."

"Agreed," he said, clasping her hand once again within his. Heat soared through him, radiating from the point of contact to the ends of his fingers and toes. He was surprised he could not see it shooting out of him like rays of light. He wanted nothing more than to gather Miss Hawkins into his arms and seal their agreement with a kiss.

She looked up into his eyes as though she might welcome just such a thing.

CHAPTER 7

Sunday dinner at the Hawkinses' house began with a squeal when Rosanna opened her parents' front door.

"Rosie, did you see?" Her youngest sister, Lottie, pressed a stack of newspapers into Rosanna's hands. "I'm a columnist. A real writer."

Her smile, so much like her sister's, spread wide and showed her teeth. Lottie's gently waving dark hair, always so much better behaved than Rosanna's, cascaded in a shining fall, loose and lovely down her back.

Rosanna took the news sheets and pretended to search for Lottie's column, flipping pages and furrowing her eyebrows.

"Rosie, you passed it," Lottie said, her voice grown quiet.

Immediately, Rosanna ended her jest. "Of course I have seen your columns. I have cut each one from the news sheets and hung it upon my wall. They're all wonderful and delicious and full of the news I love most—stories of the exhibition and all the people who attend. You should come with me next time, and we can walk through the hallways looking for interesting guests."

Lottie clapped her hands and kissed Rosanna's cheek. "Oh yes!"

"Do we get a concert before dinner?" she asked Lottie.

Her sister nodded and tucked the news sheets under one arm, holding Rosanna's waist with her other. "Ella has been warming up in the music room. Monsieur Boyé is positively wriggling on the piano bench."

Lottie's giggle was contagious, and Rosanna laughed along, trusting that the music master their parents had brought in to further Ella Hawkins's musical education continued to resemble nothing more than a stringless marionette puppet with impossibly long arms and legs.

"We ought not to make fun," Rosanna said, but then performed a flailing of her arms that parodied the music master's ritual as he took his place to accompany their sister.

At the door to the music room, the sisters quieted their laughter and entered with bright smiles and flushed cheeks.

Ella placed her violin on a table and ran to wrap her eldest sister in a hug. "It has been the longest week of my life since you were here last; I have so much to say."

Ella's voice was softer and her smile gentler than Rosanna's, but her elegance was unmatched in the family. She stood taller than either of her sisters, and though she bemoaned her too-thin frame, she was enchanting to watch with her violin in her hands. As Ella held her instrument and swayed with the music, the image suggested spring saplings in a warm breeze. Everything about Ella's playing seemed to grow out of the best parts of nature: harmonious and glorious and just a little stormy.

"I cannot wait to hear it. Tell it all," Rosanna said,

holding each sister around the waist as they came all the way into the room.

Josiah Hawkins stood from his chair, hand on his vest. "Be still my heart," he said in his deep, slow voice. "It is a trio of angels."

"Hello, Papa," Rosanna said, accepting the kiss he placed on her forehead without releasing her sisters.

"And me," Elizabeth Hawkins said, sliding into the circle of her husband and daughters.

The sweetness of the moment was not lost on Rosanna, who recalled many thorny arguments with her sisters over the years. Their mother had often scolded the sisters for fighting, telling them that they would come to regret the time they lost in disagreements, but Rosanna thought that the love they now shared was sweeter than it might have been had they never fussed and clashed. Like highlight and shadow in a painting, the remembrance of difficulties between them shed a sweet light on their current friendship.

"Ella, will you play for us now?" their father asked, gesturing for the others to take their chairs.

Ella's playing had grown masterful in the past year. The pieces she performed grew in complexity beyond Rosanna's ability to follow. She knew little of music besides the simple parlor pieces she had learned to play on the piano. Years ago, it had become clear that Ella's talents far outstripped both Rosanna's and Lottie's, and her technique only continued to improve. She could play arrangements Rosanna was certain few other violinists could match.

Today's performance was a concerto by Mozart—one of their mother's favorites.

Ella put her instrument to her shoulder and nodded to Monsieur Boyé, who flapped his arms once like a scrawny raven shaking out its wings before he played the opening notes of the accompaniment.

Rosanna stifled her grin as she avoided Lottie's eye, and they both focused on Ella's enchanting performance, from her bow work to the way her closed eyes and gentle rocking movement magnified the emotion of the piece.

Wishing she could sketch her sister's performance, Rosanna watched her with delight.

At dinner, Josiah told his daughters about a brace of pheasants that gave him quite a run, and Elizabeth detailed the new growth in her greenhouse. Each sister asked the others about their work, their practice, and their training.

"Rosanna," Elizabeth began, "when might we meet your gentleman friend?"

Rosanna sputtered a spoonful of soup. How did she know about Inspector Harrison? Her eyes darted from Lottie to Ella, neither of whom looked startled by their mother's question.

"Mrs. Ellsworth mentioned that she had met him, though she called him your 'associate,' and she said the word with the kind of smile a gossipy neighbor can never truly hide."

Elizabeth Hawkins was a woman of impeccable manners, but she did not pretend to esteem people she did not admire. Other neighbors might look down on Mrs. Ellsworth's new money, but Mrs. Hawkins did not begrudge her that; she simply did not enjoy the near-constant competition with which her neighbor approached every encounter.

"Oh," Rosanna said, a combination of relief and embarrassment coloring her cheeks. "Mr. Greystone. Of course. He does make his way into Cheetham Hill on a regular basis, but I don't know that he has done anything to deserve an introduction into our family."

Lottie swallowed a sip of her soup and said, "Might make Sunday dinner conversation more interesting."

Ella made a sound of displeasure. "We are interesting enough ourselves."

"I agree. We are quite fascinating enough to make excellent conversation," Rosanna said and hurriedly changed the subject.

Introducing Anton to her family was dangerous ground, for she would be required to know exactly how she felt about him, and she was in no way sure she understood that.

CHAPTER 8

ROSANNA KNEW MORNINGS spent in the galleries were mornings she was not painting, so she roused herself earlier every day, painting and sketching until noon. Afternoons were spent wandering the exhibition with Inspector Harrison, more often than not. She could not honestly say which she enjoyed more—the painting or the wandering.

The Gainsborough came together very nicely, sooner than she expected, which pleased Anton.

"I knew you could do it quickly, Bunny." His delight at the finished product made it easy to ignore his petulance of the past few days. He tapped the end of her nose. "You are the speediest bunny of them all."

Laughing, she said, "Of them all? Goodness. How many bunnies do you have painting for you?"

The look he gave her in response brought a lump of regret and doubt to her throat. His expression locked away and hid something as surely as a bolted door did.

Not at all sure she wanted to know his secret, she laughed again. "I am only teasing. I know I'm your girl. You've told me a hundred times," she said, allowing his arms to enfold her. Each time Anton reached for her, every conversation, all their interactions lately gave her a feeling of staleness, of insincerity.

Perhaps it was all in comparison to Mr. Harrison and the delight she felt at simply playing with him.

That was it, she realized. She and Inspector Harrison *played*. They joked, they jested, they flirted. Her face rather ached from a constant smile when they were together.

In contrast, there was no play in her relationship with Anton. At least, not play that made her feel carefree. Had there ever been? She tried to remember if she and Anton had ever bantered in the way she did with Mr. Harrison. With Martin.

But Inspector Harrison was in Manchester only on business, and only for the summer. He had told her, in one of their discussions, that this was a seasonal position and he'd be back to London when the exhibition walls came down. He would not be here forever. She'd been surprised by how sad that sentiment made her feel.

Anton was her past, her present, and her future. Her employment and her security depended on their interactions, none of which required charming flirtation. His demeanor had not changed. Anton regarded her as a treasure, as he reminded her often enough. He was affectionate, if not playful. Perhaps these lighthearted interactions with the inspector had filled a desire she did not know she had.

And so what, if Anton did not tease? If he did not play? How necessary could any of that be in a business arrangement? For what use was play, after all, in a working world?

And she was sure, now more than ever, that it was her working relationship she valued about Anton Greystone.

She wrapped the Gainsborough, Anton slipped the envelope on the table, and she opened her notebook to show him the sketches for the Michelangelo.

"And this part is left blank, like this?" he asked, his fingers almost touching her study of the painting.

"You've seen it, of course," Rosanna said. "He's sketched it in and laid in the green base-tone for skin."

Anton shook his head. "I've not seen it."

"What do you mean? This is the heart of the exhibition."

"I haven't time to spend lounging around picture halls," he said, that patronizing sneer returning to his voice, the tone that said, "Some people do nothing but gaze at paintings while the rest of us work for a living."

"Do you mean that you do not spend time at the Michelangelo, or that you do not attend the exhibit at all?"

He looked at her as though she had asked a foolish question.

When he did not answer, she prodded. "Anton?"

Shaking his head, he replied. "I have far too much work to do."

Rosanna was confused. "If you have not been visiting the exhibit, how do you decide what you want me to reproduce?"

He patted her hand. "Don't worry yourself about that."

"I do not worry myself," she said, feeling herself stiffen at yet another dismissal. "I take an interest."

"I have my people who make it their business to know what occurs on the premises."

How oppressive such a statement felt. *My people?*

Attempting to keep her voice light, she said, "Do I know these people?"

He shook his head and pulled a small book out of his breast pocket. Flipping through the pages, he said, "This little jewel has been terribly helpful." His change of the subject did not go unnoticed.

She could see half of the cover, which said, as far as she could read past his thumbs, *What to See and Where to Find It.*

She held out her hand. "May I look?"

He slipped the booklet back inside his coat, ignoring her request. "These little guides are all over the city right now. Several people who fancy themselves smarter than the rest of us are selling them. Between this"—he patted his pocket—"and my clients, I know what will sell."

Rosanna shook off her disappointment at being ignored yet again. "Have you really not been inside?"

"Never," Anton said.

"Then how do you know if my reproductions are any good?"

He turned to face her. "I know you have a great copying talent. You also have a bit of an obsession when it comes to perfection. It's what makes you a good painter."

She knew the truth of his words. She understood and agreed. Why, then, did his message sting her?

"And none of my clients have any reason to protest about *your* work. No complaints. Ever."

Had he emphasized *your* more than *work*?

Rosanna stepped close to him. "Anton, do you have

others making paintings for you?" She had never asked him directly, but lately had wondered. Never more than today.

"You, darling, are my one and only bunny." He spoke now with that oily drawl, then placed a kiss atop her hair and ran his hands down her arms.

"That is lovely of you to say, but you did not answer the question."

"You are the greatest copyist in all of England," he said, his tone practically dripping. A bit of a whine crept in as he shook his head. "My very best girl."

"Best of how many?" she asked.

He stepped back, hand to his chest as if she had shocked him. He avoided her gaze as he picked up the wrapped Gainsborough and held it close.

"Anton?" She did not back away.

Eventually he looked at her, and when he did, taking in her serious expression, his face changed.

"I hardly know what you are trying to accuse me of," he said, his voice soft and low. Dangerous, she thought. "But I hope when I return you will have remembered all that I have done for you."

He turned and left, closing the door with a soft but final click.

Staring at the door, Rosanna was speechless. What had just happened? Had she accused Anton of something so terrible? Why did it matter if he had others working for her? But if he had, why not simply say so?

For all the times he'd held her and told her she was his only "bunny" . . .

Perhaps he also held the others. Perhaps he had ridiculous names for them too.

Perhaps his kisses were no more than a function of business.

The idea had annoyed her before, but now it felt different. Only now that she had experienced an enchanting and sincere flirtation with the charming Inspector Harrison did her interactions with Anton begin to anger her.

When she thought she was the one in control of how deeply she allowed herself to feel for Anton, she knew their flirtations were a single aspect of her work. But if he was indeed sharing such attentions with other women, other painters, well, the thought made her blood run hot. It was one thing if his kisses were cursory, but another situation entirely if he was sharing them with others.

Anton Greystone was not her suitor. He was not her intended. He was nothing of the kind. But his attentions and affections had made her feel admired. Adored, even. Only now did it occur to her that she was feeling those things in vain.

Her discomfort heightened when she realized she was as guilty as she imagined Anton to be. Her flirtations with Martin Harrison were surely more heartfelt than any embrace with Greystone.

Was she as fickle and inconstant as her employer might be?

The thought made her prickle with unease.

Channeling her unsettled energy, she crossed the room to where her pewter mug filled with paintbrushes rested on the table. She lifted a board, precisely 105 by 76 centimeters, and placed it upon her largest easel. She closed her eyes and imagined each line, each fall of light, each finished and unfinished detail of Michelangelo's newly rediscovered painting.

In the following hours, her fingers worked quickly, masterfully reproducing layer after layer of what began to resemble the original in every detail. The lush reds of Mary's draped gown glowed upon the board, and as the skin tones took on the richness of life, Rosanna stepped away from the easel.

She used tempera paint, as Michelangelo had for the original, to leave the flat, rich, matte finish so often used for altar pieces. It was a different effect than oils, and it fitted the tone of the painting perfectly, placing a small distance between the subjects and the mere mortals who would come to worship before them.

Rosanna cleaned her brushes, rolling the stiffness out of her neck and shoulders that tended to come after she spent hours in the reverie that her work occasioned. She had learned of her tendency to "vacate society" while she worked when she would paint in her family's home. Her sisters would scold her for her inattention, as they could go about their work while chattering together, but Rosanna simply allowed the work to carry her away.

Only when an interruption pulled her from her trance did she pay it any mind, feeling a mental tug back to the moment at hand. She had felt such confusion when Martin Harrison had called her attention at the exhibition. Now that she thought back to it, he had appeared somewhat worried as she dragged herself out of her dreamy state.

Perhaps her reveries were more noticeable than she imagined.

Anton called it a stupor, but she felt anything but stupid while she worked. Unconscious of what passed about her, perhaps, but infinitely aware of what was occurring within her: the minuscule effects and changes that her pencils, pens, and brushes made. She felt no hunger, no sleepiness. Her arms could carry on for hours, led by the image burned into her memory.

Only after she stopped working did her body remind her to eat or rest.

Even as her stomach growled, she remembered she and Lottie were meeting at the exhibition to discuss one of the paintings Lottie wanted to highlight in her column.

Rosanna pulled off her work dress and apron, now spattered with paint, and dressed in her most flattering blue-and-green plaid. Because, she thought, she should look her best to meet her sister. The thought made her grin. The smile remained while she checked her face in the glass, tucking her escaping curls back into their knot. Of course the effort was all for her sister.

Helping herself to cold beef and bread from Mrs. Whitmore's larder, Rosanna ate lunch as she made her way toward the exhibition, telling herself that after she met with Lottie, she would study the etchings again. Perhaps what she needed was a fresh look. As the Rembrandts seemed impossible, she could attempt to recreate one of Durer's or Vandyck's.

And if she happened to come across any other interesting paintings, or interesting people, so much the better.

Lottie stood near the front entrance of the exhibition, pencil in one hand, notebook in the other. Rosanna watched her sister's gaze sweep across the crowd until it locked onto something interesting, and without moving her eyes to her notebook, Lottie scribbled line after line.

Rosanna walked toward her sister, realizing that was a trait all three Hawkins sisters shared: they could maintain focus on an object with their eyes, and use their hands at the same time to represent it—Lottie with words, Rosanna with images, and Ella with music.

Rosanna was inches away from Lottie before her sister noticed her.

Lottie leaned her face close to her sister and allowed Rosanna to place a kiss on her cheek as she finished writing a line. Tucking her pencil into her notebook, she placed them both in her small bag, neatly putting her work away. Rosanna self-consciously patted at her hair, a nest of pencils and brushes bristling from her curls, and wished she could maintain such an organized state as she walked through the exhibition.

Lottie pulled Rosanna to a portrait of a sea captain, his vessel in the background.

"Do you think we could make a story of this?" Lottie asked.

Rosanna tugged at her sister's arm, entwined with hers. "Do you not believe we could make a story of any painting?"

The sisters laughed.

Rosanna asked, "Why this one, particularly? There is not much significant artistic merit here, I think."

Lottie shook her head, her grin deepening. "Artistic merit is fine, but look at him. He's terribly agreeable, is he not?"

With a humming sound, Rosanna nodded. "Oh, I daresay any naval captain with such a gravely studious look has a delightful personality."

Lottie laughed. "As though you could look away should he step out of that painting and stand before you."

Rosanna nodded. "I see what we are discussing. Agreeable to *look at*. I shan't argue with that. He is rather finer than most men one sees in Manchester."

With a sigh, Lottie squinted at the painting. "I believe he and I would suit perfectly."

"In which case, you ought to write an article about this painting in hopes that the model appears, clutching your news sheet, demanding to meet the woman who sees him so clearly."

"You understand me perfectly," Lottie said with a laugh, pressing her sister's arm.

As they turned from the painting, Lottie whispered into Rosanna's ear, "Speaking of men who could have stepped out of a painting." She gestured with her chin to the gallery to their right. "I'll take the sailor; you can have the Peeler."

Rosanna glanced in the direction her sister indicated. Martin Harrison strode through the gallery, his hands clasped at his back, looking both alert and relaxed. With all her self-control, Rosanna stifled a laugh and pulled Lottie into the gallery toward Mr. Harrison.

Lottie tugged Rosanna's arm. "No. Don't. I was only

jesting. We have outgrown this game, Rosie." Her last words came out as a combined plea and hiss.

"Beg your pardon, Inspector," Rosanna said as they reached Martin's side. "I wonder if you could assist us."

He turned, and as soon as he saw Rosanna, his face bloomed into a delighted smile. "If at all possible, miss," he said with a bow.

"This young lady," she said, gesturing to Lottie, "wonders if you could help her find someone."

Mr. Harrison turned to Lottie. "Have you become separated from your party?" he asked, looking ready and eager to assist.

Lottie hissed, "Rosie, no."

Rosanna ignored her sister. "If I describe someone, can you tell us if you've seen him?"

Inspector Harrison looked back to Rosanna, a half-smile on his face. "I can try."

"He is an upright, tall gentleman. A naval man in uniform. His face is handsome—would you call it *very* handsome, Lottie?" she asked. "Or *extremely* handsome?"

Lottie shouldered her way in front of Rosanna to speak to the inspector. "I apologize, sir. My sister is unwell. She has been let out, only for today, from her locked cell where she will certainly return soon. We do not mean to waste your time."

"Your sister?" he said. "How delightful. A pleasure to meet you, Miss Hawkins." He offered his hand.

Lottie stood between them, mouth open.

Rosanna took Lottie's hand and placed it in his offered

one. "Inspector Harrison, may I present my youngest sister? Lottie, this is Inspector Harrison."

Recovering quickly, Lottie said, "It is a pleasure to meet any friend of Rosie's. And a comfort to know that there is a professional nearby should she lose what remains of her mind altogether." She batted Rosanna's arm. "Silly."

Mr. Harrison's eyes danced as he glanced from one sister to the other. "Have you really lost a gentleman?"

"No, but we would appreciate hearing of anyone answering that description," Rosanna said. "Lottie is always on the lookout."

Laughing, Lottie shook her head. "You make me sound like such an intelligent, charming woman of substance. I thank you to stop now."

Rosanna shook her head. "I am only just beginning."

Lottie gave Rosanna's hand a gentle pinch. Rosanna grinned back at her.

After a glance at Inspector Harrison, Lottie said, "What will this gentleman think of us?" with an impeccable impression of their grandmother's disapproving gaze.

He broke in with a short laugh. "I have had ample time over the past few weeks to make up my mind about Miss Hawkins." Then he ducked his head and continued, "And I am always happy to add to my previous impressions."

"And that," Lottie said, "is my cue to withdraw." She turned to the inspector. "A pleasure to meet you, sir." Turning back to Rosanna, she leaned in and kissed her cheek. "Keep an eye out for the naval captain. See you Sunday," she said, and with a wink, she walked away.

Rosanna loved so much about her sister, but her understanding of when to make an exit was on top of the list.

She smiled at Inspector Harrison, pleased to both give and receive full attention. He appeared equally delighted.

The feeling that overcame her in the presence of Martin Harrison was golden sunlight as opposed to the charcoal shadow of her morning's interaction with Anton Greystone. Chiaroscuro. Light and shade.

"Miss Hawkins, I was hoping to see you today," the inspector said, the smile on his face bare of even a trace of Anton's brand of oiliness.

"Were you?" she asked, ducking her head with a hint of embarrassment for her silliness with Lottie. "I am happy to be able to fulfill your wishes."

"I find that all my days are better when you appear," he said, a slow flush joining the smile on his face.

Rosanna wondered if he recalled, as she did, each of their meetings.

He offered his arm, and she took it, enjoying his calm assurance. His confidence, polite and attentive, invited her to feel a measure of her own.

Such a welcome change from Anton's patronizing manner of speaking to her, which served rather to sap her self-assurance. She was capable to produce, she knew. But with Anton Greystone, her ability to do, to make, to generate was all she felt confident in; never to become, to deserve, or to simply exist.

This inspector granted Rosanna the pleasure of feeling worthy to take up space. To be allowed to be in the universe without paying a fee for the privilege.

"What are you thinking about?" Mr. Harrison asked. "Your sister?"

Rosanna laughed. "Not my sister, though she is charming. No, nothing worth speaking aloud. And you?" She could feel the flush of heat rising in her face. What a relief he could not have guessed where her silly thoughts were taking her.

"There's a painting I want to ask you about," he said, leading her to the gallery displaying most of the modern, local artists. She had spent very little time here, and she was surprised to find high-quality pieces among them, including several interesting landscapes and seascapes as well as a pretty view of a manor nearly obscured by trees.

She was happy to wander slowly through the gallery, knowing that none of the paintings would draw the attention of Anton Greystone or his clients. She didn't have to memorize them and could simply enjoy the artwork.

Mr. Harrison led her to a painting of a young couple gazing at each other, their faces filling most of the frame.

"Why does this picture surprise me?" he asked.

"What do you mean?" she asked, unable to take her eyes from the image. She felt surprised herself, and she loved the feeling.

He made a humming sound, as if he were pondering how to clarify his question. "I feel something different looking at this painting than I do about others. As though I'm . . . intruding."

She smiled. Still staring at the faces in the painting, she squeezed his arm and said, "That is precisely it. We are intruding."

"But why?" he asked. "I do not mean to be difficult, Miss Hawkins. I only wonder why this piece gives me that impression—gives us that impression," he clarified, and she felt a shiver of happiness that they experienced this moment together.

She pulled her eyes from the painting.

"I think I know," she said. "Is there somewhere we can go to be alone for a few moments?"

She saw the effect her words had on him, his initial shock at her suggestion and the slow building smile.

"I believe I know a place," he said, his eyes dancing.

He led her to a small wing lined with office doors. Opening one and gesturing her inside, he stepped in after her.

"Shall I close the door, Miss Hawkins?"

She shook her head. "For the purposes of artistic instruction, I believe that might be best, but I have a reputation to protect."

He put his back to the open door and turned to her, smiling.

My, but he was handsome.

"Right. Now, when you've looked at portraits, how do you most often see the subject?" she asked, noticing how much she sounded like a strict governess.

He must have heard a similar note, for he sounded shy when he said, "I am not sure."

"Have you perhaps noticed," she said, trying for a less teacherly tone, "how most of the subjects of paintings appear with their faces either turned toward you, the viewer, or slightly to one side?"

She moved to stand so he could see her at full-face and then at a three-quarter view.

"Right. Yes, now that you mention it."

"I believe this gives us, the viewer, certain impressions." She felt excited to share this thought with him, and he looked as eager to hear what she had to say. They could have held this discussion amidst the crowds of the exhibition, but she knew what was coming, which was why she asked for the privacy of this small room.

"When we focus on a subject straight on, we feel we are interacting with him or her. There is a level at which you can, in fact, meet the gaze. Do you know this feeling?" she asked, hoping she was not overstretching his understanding. As she spoke, she moved slowly, and his eyes followed hers as she hoped they would.

He nodded. "Of course. Sometimes it seems the paintings are watching me." He ducked his head as though embarrassed by his confession.

She laughed. "That is delightful. It shows that you have a very fine sense of community within these walls. Many of the subjects of these paintings shall soon be your friends."

"Some of them are far too frightening to wish as friends," he said, joining her laugh.

"When a subject is looking slightly to one side," she said, tilting her head partially away from him, "do you see how you become somewhat distant from the moment? More an observer than a participant?"

He seemed to think for a moment. "I believe I shall notice it now, when I look at them again," he said, and she nodded.

She loved the openness with which he listened and absorbed her words. As though what she had to say to him was important.

"There are many paintings here in the galleries and halls wherein the subjects are locked in embraces, whether violent or loving." She saw his cheeks redden again. "But generally, at least one of them still faces the viewer. The painting you showed me just now presents a different aspect. As though the painter had not asked them to pose for him but instead had interrupted a private moment."

She stood directly before him.

"Look into my eyes, Inspector," she said. Her request sounded more like a demand, so she shook her head and tried again. "I beg your pardon. If you please, sir, try this with me."

He made no objection. Standing close, he looked down at her. She tilted her chin to meet his eyes.

"I propose that it would be difficult to hold each other's eyes for many long minutes. Yet a painter might need his subjects to remain in a pose for hours, days even." As she spoke, the warmth of his gaze settled upon her, making it difficult to summon the words she wanted to say.

"I . . ." she began, as her breath fled, leaving her unsure of the word she intended to say next. "I believe," she said, her words a mere whisper, "when we looked upon the subjects, we *were* intruding upon an intimate moment."

He did not take his eyes from hers.

She found it difficult to swallow.

"Can you imagine," she whispered, "holding this glance for much longer without moving?"

He took a small step closer to her, halving the distance between them.

"I cannot," he said, his voice tremulous.

She felt his hand upon her arm before she realized he had taken yet another step forward. The heat of his touch burned through her sleeve, but their eyes remained locked together.

"I do feel," he said, his words hardly more than a breath, "that I know you better now than I did only moments ago."

"And so," she said, barely able to stand for the trembling of her knees, "can you see how difficult a pose"—why was it so hard to breathe?—"this might be"—she reached her own hand to his arm to steady herself—"to maintain?"

Every nerve in her body sang with sparks. Her hand upon his arm clutched the sleeve of his jacket in a reflexive action she could not have controlled.

"Impossible," he responded, drawing his hand from her shoulder to the side of her face, cupping her cheek within his warm fingers.

He moved his hand tenderly until his fingertips grazed the back of her neck. Every strand of hair, every cell of her skin came alive at his touch.

She could not have said with any certainty who moved first or if they simply came together at the same moment, but when his lips touched hers, she felt the delicious sensation of simultaneously falling and floating. Her legs could no longer support her, but she felt as if she could never fall as long as he held her.

She reached her arms about his neck, returning pressure for pressure, tenderness for tenderness. As his arms wrapped solidly around her, she saw firelight behind her eyes, sparks of gold and blue, heat and warmth made visible by the touch of his mouth on hers.

Had anything ever felt so lovely, so perfect?

CHAPTER 9

HAD ANY WOMAN EVER been so lovely, so perfect?

Martin drew back enough so he could look upon her face. Eyes still closed, her lashes settled against flushed cheeks, she appeared like a sleepy angel. He leaned forward again and placed a kiss upon both of her eyelids.

She took in a gentle breath, and he felt his heartbeat settle into a rhythm at once new and familiar.

"Rosanna," he whispered. "May I call you Rosanna?"

She opened her eyes and met his gaze. "I believe you have earned the right to such informality, sir," she said, her teasing grin adding to her beauty.

"Martin, please," he said.

"Martin, please," she repeated, more of a plea than a simple repetition, and in answer, he placed another kiss upon her lips.

"Martin, I thank you," she said, her face aglow.

"I wish I could paint," he said, his eyes taking in every aspect of her face. "I should like to put this exact expression in a portrait for all time." His fingers drew the softest line across her cheek, down her nose, along her full lips. "But I would keep it where only I could see it."

She smiled up at him again. "That strikes me as perfectly selfish, sir. What is art for if not to be shared?"

He could not answer in the same teasing tone; he felt too much. "Then perhaps I am glad I have no such talent. I shall, instead, hold the memory of your face within my mind and heart forever." The words fell from his lips as a whisper, and he saw her accept them with a gentle sigh.

She moved to look about the office: small desk, uncomfortable wooden chair, bare walls. "Is this where you do your important inspecting, Martin?"

Surely she knew what the sound of his name in her voice was doing to him.

He shook his head. "I have the privilege of wandering the galleries. As it happens, all the daily security protocols keep things running perfectly, and I rarely have reason to come in here."

"I am glad to hear it. I fear if this room reflected your personality, it would tell a rather bleak story." She ran her finger along the edge of the desk, landing on the thin sheaf of papers detailing the queen's imminent visit.

Which gave him an idea.

"Rosanna," he said, "I wonder if I could ask you something."

She turned the fullness of her smile upon him. "Anything, as long as you keep calling me by my name."

He chuckled to think they each received this small attention with the same eagerness.

"Would you accompany me on a tour around the exhibition on Tuesday of next week?"

She put her hands behind her and leaned against the desk. "Do I not accompany you around today? And so many other days?"

"You do. And I am always grateful. Possibly more today than any day before," he said, feeling delightfully wicked when he saw how his words brought the blush back to her cheeks. "But there is a particular reason I hope for your company Tuesday."

She tilted her head as if she could never grow tired of hearing him speak. Had anyone ever listened to him with such thoughtfulness? Had he ever desired it so much?

"There is a very special guest coming to Manchester on Tuesday," he went on. "I shall be required to attend this guest here but also to keep a respectful distance, as well as to keep others from crowding in."

"Goodness," she said, her eyebrows raised and her hand pressed to her heart. "Someone has very particular needs. Who is this person?"

With a shrug, he made a noise of disinterest. "Lady called Victoria."

A burst of delighted laughter escaped from Rosanna, and Martin was sure he had never heard anything that pleased him so much. Except for his name on her lips. And perhaps her lips on his lips.

"Victoria? Queen Victoria?" Rosanna was impressed, that much was clear.

Martin nodded. "The very same."

Another smile grew upon her mouth. "And should I be able to meet her? Speak with her?"

"Honestly, I do not know." Martin had not yet met with the queen's man, of course, so he was unsure about Her Majesty's wishes. "One hears she is a charming and delightful sort of person, but I imagine it would be nice for her to simply attend an event without having the public make an affair of it."

Rosanna nodded. "I shan't make an affair, I promise. I shall determine to be pleased if only I can catch a glimpse of her. Or perhaps follow at a few discretionary paces."

"I would love to have you here," Martin said.

"I have questions," she said.

He nodded for her to ask them.

"What should a woman attending the security detail wear in the presence of royalty? I would never wish to offend." Her grin suggested she had no real concern on this point.

"I promise to find you uncommonly lovely no matter what you wear."

"Plaid, I think," she said, nodding thoughtfully and glancing at her skirts. "Scottish fabrics shall never go out of fashion now that Balmoral Castle is the kingdom's premier travel destination."

"I trust you know what you are talking about," he said, unable to take his eyes from her. "Have you another question for me?"

She nodded, a solemn look crossing her face.

He wondered if she was somehow hurt or offended.

She placed her hands on her tiny waist and tilted her

head. "What is to stop you, on the coming Tuesday, from pulling me into an office and kissing me dizzy?"

He had no idea how to answer that question, so he asked one of his own. "Are you dizzy, Rosanna?"

She stepped closer. "Not at the moment, but I believe you know how to solve that problem."

He did indeed. Wrapping his arms about her, he pulled her to him. As their lips met again, he felt her smile against his own.

No kiss had ever felt so natural, so filled with promise and delight. So much more wonderful than his childish blundering and shy glances of years past.

She broke from him and leaned back to look into his face. "You are very good at this," she said, laughing.

To kiss a woman who knew what she wanted and had no fear of speaking her wish? Bliss.

"I was thinking the same about you," he replied.

"It appears we make an excellent team. But I believe it is time for us to make our way back into the galleries," she said. "There must be more paintings that need to be discovered, explored, and explained."

The very thought brought Martin a sense of great joy.

As they wandered through galleries large and small, arm in arm, Rosanna pointed out important pieces to him.

"This is widely thought to be the best portrait of Queen Mary," she said. "Although I believe she looks as if she suffers from a toothache."

He could not argue.

"See how the artist has tucked a flower into her hand?

Each plant holds meaning, but I don't know what. I imagine someone here could tell us the significance."

"Or you could make something up," Martin said with a smile.

"Indeed, I could. But it would mean very little to me if I invented it. I should like to see a painting of our Queen Victoria clutching a kitchen knife, or perhaps a croquet mallet, looking ready to whack a ball through a wicket." Her face lit up with delight. "Don't you think that would give a more interesting idea of what she was like than, say, a sprig of rosemary?"

Anything would sound interesting when it was said by this woman.

"Does our queen play croquet?" Martin asked.

"Doesn't everyone?"

Rosanna Hawkins was by far the most charming woman in the world.

"Perhaps Her Majesty would let you paint her," Martin said. "With or without lawn skittles."

Rosanna laughed, but he caught a look of longing in her eyes.

They rounded another corner and came face to face with a portly monarch covered in jewels and furs.

"That," she said, "is Holbein's *King Henry VIII*. It's not the original, though. Doesn't he look pleased with himself?"

"He certainly does. Wait," he said as she began to lead him past. "This is a copy?" He leaned in to look closely, as though perhaps he might be able to tell.

"A replica. Making replicas is how people learn to paint.

Many famous pieces have museum reproductions made," she said. "In fact—"

"That is dreadful."

"Is it?" She looked surprised. "Why?"

Did he really need to explain? "What is the purpose of a priceless and original work of art if one can simply make a copy?"

He did not truly expect her to answer, but she did.

"Protection, for one. Had this museum reproduction never been made, when the original painting caught fire, all record of it would have been gone forever."

Martin shook his head. "Perhaps it should be, then."

"I doubt Henry would agree." She gave a small laugh but shook her head. "Also, who is to decide that only the blessed few should have access to great art? If a piece exists only in a private collection, it remains hidden from the world."

Of course. Such a thing was obvious.

He nodded. "That is what museums are for. And exhibitions like this one."

She gave him another small smile. "Lucky for us, then, that we happen to live in Manchester at this time. What of those who never leave their small villages? What of the poor Americans? What have they to look at but each other?"

Now he was sure she was teasing. He felt the need to underscore the seriousness of his opinion. "I should be sorry to think that any great works were being copied simply to cover wall space in a wealthy man's home. If I have learned anything from this summer's experience being surrounded by priceless masterpieces, it is that some things are best in the original." He shook his head. "Something about the very idea of making imitations of the great paintings feels . . . unlawful."

When she answered, her voice was quiet, a brittle tone behind it. "Perhaps that is the policeman in you speaking. Most people would probably not be so quick to call an innocent artistic undertaking *unlawful*." She led him on to the next painting in the gallery.

"Perhaps it is the inspector in me, but in my experience, there is nothing innocent about criminal behavior."

She scoffed, a somewhat bitter laugh. "Surely you don't mean criminal?"

"No, that is exactly what I mean. Forgery is criminal."

"Forgery?" She sounded shocked, as though she had forgotten what had prompted the topic.

He simply nodded.

She did not reply, did not speak for many minutes. She turned her face from him, perhaps in study of the paintings they passed, or perhaps by her design.

"Rosanna, have I offended you?" he asked, sure he was misinterpreting her silence.

"Indeed not, Inspector Harrison." She faced him, but the smile she presented was nothing like those easy grins and sighs of only the hour earlier. It was stiff, forced, and, he could not help but think, unhappy. "You are the expert on legal matters."

"And you are the expert on artistic ones," he said, hoping to coax a more sincere smile.

She responded with only a humming sound of assent.

Something was wrong. He felt the stiffness, the chill in her demeanor, and he knew he was at fault. Somehow she seemed not to understand precisely how he could recognize the criminal aspect of a faked painting.

Could he tell her?

Would she listen? Would she understand if he opened this terrible door and let her see his dark secret?

She continued to walk away, and he knew he needed to tell her. He must.

"Rosanna," he said. "Please wait a moment."

She paused but did not turn around.

"You seem out of sorts, and I take the blame for that." He found it difficult to swallow. "I must explain something to you, if you will hear me."

She moved slowly, turning to meet his eyes, and he felt the weight of her gaze: patient, but not intimate.

"My father," he began, and then coughed. In a softer register, he continued to speak. "My father was involved in criminal undertakings," he said, hoping that the barest of facts could help her see.

She didn't say anything.

"The shame of his behavior shadowed my mother and me for all our lives." His voice sank lower, and he had a moment to wonder if she could hear him. "I cannot justify any such behavior. Not in anyone."

With all his heart, he hoped she would say something, would communicate that she understood his pain and could forgive him for his connections.

She did not speak, nor did she look at him again as they walked toward the entry doors.

He resolved to say nothing more—she deserved time to process this shameful information. He could be patient.

When they arrived at the entrance hall, Rosanna slipped her arm from his. "I must be on my way," she said, managing to lift her mouth into a more credible smile. "I thank you for a lovely day."

"I am sorry I brought darkness into it," he said, unable to meet her eye.

He wanted to ask her to stay, to take her into his arms again, to repair whatever damage he had done by his confession. In the busy vestibule, however, he simply took her hand and raised it to his lips.

"It was the most wonderful day I can remember," he said, hoping she could hear his sincerity. "I thank you for spending it with me."

Was there a tear in her eye? She turned from him.

"Rosanna?" he said. "Are you well?"

She turned back, a half-smile on her lips. "Do you know you ask me that question quite often?" She raised her hand in a wave and slipped away through the crowd.

Why, he wondered, did he feel a stab of apprehension? They had spent a perfect afternoon in delicious company together. Certainly, all was well. She would be forgiving, would she not? What else was there to fear?

MANCHESTER HERALD-TRIBUNE

June 24, 1857

Official Visit to the Art Treasures Exhibition

Lottie Hawkins

If the reader is planning an outing to the Art Treasures Exhibition within the next week, this reporter feels compelled to suggest that such a visit take place early in the week, for whispers of a royal guest are already circulating through the city.

We cannot confirm that Her Royal Highness Queen Victoria will make an official state visit, but the bustlings of preparations are being overheard. Exhibition committee members are in a dither, rushing here and there inside the halls. Unofficial word is spreading. Many suppositions, many rumors. Not that we at the *Herald-Tribune* give credence to rumor.

However, some rumor carries more weight, and therefore begs more likely acceptance. For such reasons, this journalist recommends keeping a watchful eye Monday and Tuesday.

Shall the queen wander through the exhibit halls, pointing out images of family members from generations past? Shall she choose a particular favorite and stand before it, watching the light change through the day? Might you, reader, catch a royal glimpse?

This writer suggests that if you see a stately but unassuming woman surrounded by guards and officers, you ought to keep your distance but capture the moment in your memory. For who knows how long it might be before our city is once again graced with such an illustrious visit?

CHAPTER 10

STRIDING OUT OF THE exhibit hall and stomping down the path, Rosanna pressed against the hordes of people entering. She welcomed the jostling of the throng; she needed to get away from Inspector Martin Harrison, and what better way to disappear than into a crowd?

How dare he? How dare he accuse her of such things? Even had he only whispered the suggestion that mimicry was distasteful, she would have felt hurt. But he went too far. Accusing her—or at least people like her—of forgery and criminal intent? Even if he did not know he was talking about her, the suggestion stung. And from him, of all people. He ought to know better, having been raised by someone who had created their family's wealth through crime.

"Do I look like a criminal?" she said aloud, causing several heads to turn in her direction.

A man's voice called back, "Not much."

She ignored the people she passed and continued to push toward home.

Rosanna knew little to nothing about police work,

and her interactions with Martin had not shown her much about his profession. Did his career consist solely of strolling through galleries with her on his arm, listening to her silly ramblings? Making circuits of the exhibition and occasionally breaking up large groups or asking people to take a step back from a painting? If that was his idea of meaningful employment, how could he venture to form an opinion about hers? She worked hard. And she was very good at her job.

Her dedication, her study, her natural ability, and her hours, months, and years of practice had seen to her success.

What did he know about art, in any case?

He could not even see the artistic merit in Michelangelo. What kind of a person scoffed at Michelangelo?

But he had surprised her today with his reaction to the portrait of the two young lovers.

Now why, she wondered, did she assume the subjects of that painting were lovers?

Of course, she knew why. Now more than ever. For who could hold such an intimate gaze and not grow close?

She had been foolish to recreate such a moment with Inspector Harrison. She practically threw herself at him, inviting herself into his deserted office. What would her mother say? She shook her head; she knew exactly what her mother would say.

Naturally he responded as he did. How could he do otherwise? With a bit of attraction, which she knew they both felt, such dedicated moments of silent staring into each other's eyes must bring them into the next level of attraction.

And that kiss. Those kisses.

They were lovely, wonderful.

But then he proved how little they could possibly understand one another. She had watched him calm small scuffles in the galleries, had witnessed him removing a small and sticky child from a too-close proximity to a sculpture. Now each of these actions, and all those like them, felt not only careful, but judgmental. It was short work in her mind to move him from judgmental to critical, from critical to unforgiving.

He did not even seem to have forgiven his own father. Had he told her that story so she would understand that she could not be expected to feel any mercy from him? His rigid sense of rightness, of correctness, of suitability, and more to the point, his effortless categorization of her work as criminal, lawless, and wicked, pained her deeply. Was she a source of shame to Inspector Harrison now, as truly as was his father?

She had spent hours in his company; how could they understand each other so little?

And why, she asked herself, should it matter so terribly?

When the exhibition closed in autumn and his work took him away, she would never see Inspector Martin Harrison again. And now that she understood how ill-suited they were to one another, all the better.

But that kiss . . .

Never had a kiss struck her with such force, such passion. Anton Greystone's infrequent and inconsistent attentions, coupled with his tendency to speak endearments that made her cringe instead of swoon, had never elicited a response in her such as she had felt today.

She raised her hands to her cheeks, remembering Martin's touch, as gentle as a breeze. But when he had wrapped her in his arms, she had slipped into the blissful surrender to his strength.

Fisting her hands, she straightened her arms at her sides. No more. Never again would she allow herself to be fooled by Mr. Martin Harrison's touch, his glance, or his smile. He may kiss like a lover, but he judged like a Peeler.

She would remind herself of his malformed and inflexible opinions. Often, and loudly, if needed. But perhaps, she thought, not as she walked through the streets of Manchester.

Rosanna Hawkins was a painter. It was what she was born to do. Her work made her who she was. She loved seeing the pieces come together under her fingers. Hands without pencils and paintbrushes seemed not her own hands at all.

Any person, no matter how handsome or charming he might appear, who tried to deny her gifts or dissuade her from practicing them, must be avoided.

❧

Rosanna's mind had cleared on the walk back to her room, and she knew what she had to do. She would work while the light remained, and after that, if needed, she would light every candle at her disposal.

It was time to perfect the Michelangelo reproduction.

She pulled out the three remaining prepared boards and placed them side by side on her easels, two freestanding with long legs, and one on a tabletop. With her pencil, she drew in the outlines of each figure, first on one board, then the next, and the next. When she was satisfied that each line was perfect, she prepared her paints. Laying in the undertones for each figure, her hands worked independent of her thoughts.

Characters on the far left—greenish undertones and nothing more. The unfinished "final" product already showing. Moving to the middle of the painting, she blocked Mary's undertones onto the first board, then upon another board, and then the last. Then small Jesus, followed by the little John, and at last, the two angel figures on the right.

Next: another layer of skin tone, dabbling the tempera paint in layers to unlock the richness of the medium. Golden skin, dazzling robes, as much light and shadow as the incomplete final product allowed.

As Rosanna worked, stroke after touch after detail, her anger melted into acceptance, both in the realm of her work and her heart. As each section of each reproduction came closer to life, she felt more resolved.

This was who she was. Rosanna Hawkins was a painter. A talented, prolific reproductionist. That would never change, but what might change could be the scale and scope of her projects.

Anton Greystone was not the only person in this partnership capable of selling her paintings.

She was certain she could sell her own work to Mrs. Ellsworth, and knowing how competitive the fast-growing wealthy set were, Rosanna felt confident others would follow Mrs. Ellsworth's example. And if Rosanna were the seller rather than Anton, she could charge a lower price. The sale would only need provide for one person's income, after all.

A smile played at her lips as she considered the possibility.

She touched the black paint to the edges of Mary's robes, the place she was certain would have been a rich aquamarine had the painting been finished. It made sense compositionally, and she could see it in her mind.

At the same moment, a different image flashed into her inner eye: the glint of light off a burnished halo.

There was no lack of gilded halos in Renaissance art, and the religious painting masters had created many effective representations of light, internal or external, shining both onto and from the ever-present halos.

Rosanna lifted her brush from the painting. She stared at the boards in front of her but didn't see them.

Instead, she saw in her mind a ray of sunshine illuminating a gold ring, then a pool of still water, and then a child's soft skin. In an instant, each of the images settled into her mind with a foundationally similar impression: capturing the light was not a matter of exact representation, but rather a condition of sensation. Image after image flooded her internal sight, not of light as it *was*, but of light as it *felt*.

Winking, sparkling, warm.

The light she saw in her heart, not only with her eyes.

Color and texture not as they looked exactly but as they

tasted. As they sounded. As they felt against her skin. As they came alive through her brushes.

She allowed her eyes to close as she inhaled once and then exhaled, long and slow, savoring the feeling that overcame her as she contemplated her wish to share this experience.

Then she opened her eyes, shook her head, and continued to work.

Impossible.

Each of her previous attempts to transfer those irrational impressions had met only with contempt.

Ridiculous.

That was the word her masters had used. At least, that was the most delicate of the descriptions. She knew it was true. Art ought to reflect what one could see. Her notions of the taste of candlelight or the scent of the glint of sunrise on the water could not translate through words let alone through paint, so how could she blame anyone for not understanding what she meant?

These small digressions from her daily work had come more often this summer, as she had studied and reproduced so many masterful pieces. Images of how things might be, as opposed to how they were, shot into her mind unbidden, much as they had when she was a student, when her masters made no secret of the inappropriateness of attempting to put such images on canvas or paper.

There was no place for such things in painting, but she was discovering that if she fought against them, they would wake her from deep sleep and not allow her to rest.

If, however, she allowed the phantasms of light to come, stay a moment, and then leave, she could set the ideas aside and return to her work. With no real notion of what caused these momentary interruptions, she had decided to accept them as they came; surely it happened to all painters. It was natural to see glimpses of unreality when days passed filled with the act of reproducing exact images. One's mind simply grew tired.

All right then, she told herself with a shake of her head. *Back to the Michelangelo.*

When her candles began to gutter, she saw with delight that she had come farther than she'd hoped.

A small meal and a decent night of rest would do her a world of good. She bid good night to the works in progress, pushing any intruding thoughts of both Anton Greystone and Martin Harrison firmly out of her mind.

Morning brought weak, leaden light through her small window. Rain. A perfect excuse to stay in all day and work.

She could not regret the added incentive to stay away from the exhibition. A sleep filled with dreams of Martin Harrison had been no help at all when it came to steeling her resolve against the impudent man and his self-righteous inferences about painting and, in all probability, many other things he knew little or nothing about.

Dressing quickly and donning an apron, she began work early and stayed at it for hours, allowing the repetitive nature of her painting to soothe her frazzled nerves. The work was demanding, but she was up to the task, filled with both confidence and delight.

The dim light leaking through the clouds gave a different ambience to her paintings' details. She felt wrapped in the safety of her warm room as rain pounded against the roof and walls and occasional thunder added to the muffled rumblings.

At a knock at the door, she stiffened. She had not wanted Anton to see today's work, so she had taken the extra precaution of barring the door, which she generally did not do.

"Bunny, have you locked me out?" came Anton's wheedling voice.

"In a moment," she called back to him.

She placed two of the Michelangelo reproduction boards in her bedroom and closed the door, rearranging the two that remained: one from her first attempt, and another from last night's working session that had spilled over into this morning.

"Do let me inside, or Mrs. Whitmore might toss me out into the rain. It's wet as Noah today," he said.

Rosanna unlocked the door and was greeted by Anton's dripping hat as he handed it to her.

"What have you got to show me today?" he asked, bypassing his occasional insincere chatter. Perhaps he wanted to avoid a revisiting of their last conversation and any additional probing questions she might have about the nature of his business and other employees, particularly any questions about his relationships with the women in his employ.

As such thoughts crossed her mind, Rosanna realized she no longer cared how many painters Anton had hired. He could have an entire fleet of them, and he could give a patronizing animal name and a kiss to each of them.

It did not matter to her at all. She was unattached to Anton, either as an employer or as a beau. Let Inspector Martin Harrison think what he would; her work was as legitimate as anyone else's, and she would own the entire process, beginning to end. Let Anton complain; she was her own best advocate, and she would do what she pleased. Anton's choices would no longer affect her.

She led him to the two easels holding the Michelangelo images. He walked around them, peering at the detail, then nodded, smiling appreciatively at her.

She smiled back and meant it. She was glad he was pleased. She wanted him to be happy with this painting, for this was her last piece for Anton Greystone. She was finished with him.

"How soon?" he asked.

She flinched, wondering if he somehow knew what she was thinking, but then she realized he meant how soon he could expect this piece to be finished.

"Before the week's end, I trust." Stepping between him and the boards, she said, "You can see that this one is farther along, but the quality of the other is slightly truer to the original."

"I'll take them both, of course," he said.

She shook her head. "I think I shall keep one."

He laughed, and she wondered how she had ever thought that sound to be something other than cruel.

"What would you do with it?" he asked, gesturing first at

the reproduction and then along her walls. "Do you think it enhances the aesthetic of your apartments?"

How was it possible that she had allowed him to speak to her in such a way for so long? To allow herself to believe he was right to do so?

"I think beautiful art reflects beauty on any space wherein it resides," she said, remaining calm and standing tall.

He sneered again. "Indeed." She understood he meant the opposite. "Well, then, I shall be back on Saturday for the most accurate reproduction. You cannot grudge me the first pick."

"Of course you shall have your choice," Rosanna said.

"And the etchings?" he prompted.

"I have had little luck with the Rembrandt etchings. Once this is complete to my satisfaction," she said, gesturing to the *Madonna*, "I shall attempt to reproduce the Durer or the Vandyck."

He shook his head. "Rembrandt will sell better."

"But not if it appears crooked or imbalanced," she countered. "If you have another worker better able to create the etchings, I suggest you use her."

He stepped closer, reaching his hand to hold her by the shoulder. The touch felt more restraining than tender. "Are we going to do this again?" He turned her to face him. "There is no one like you. No one."

She met his eyes, her gaze steady. "Of course. But if someone *not like me* can pull off the Rembrandt, you ought to encourage her."

Anton attempted to pull Rosanna close to him, but she stepped out of his embrace. "If I am to have this ready for transportation by Saturday, I must give it my full attention. Thank you for coming by," she said, gesturing to the door.

Her back was turned as it clicked behind him, and she released her breath.

CHAPTER 11

AS MARTIN STALKED THE galleries and hallways of the exhibition, seeking out trouble and finding none, he could not help but question what had happened with Miss Hawkins.

Rosanna.

It had been days, and she had not come back.

Had she not felt the same effect of their kisses as he had? Was he perhaps mistaken about their attraction?

He had experienced, for the moments they had spent together, a surety found nowhere else in his life. She responded and guided him in every way as a woman feeling the flush of love.

He was not mistaken. Their attraction was real.

But something had sent her away. Something had stopped her from coming back.

Were they victims of poor timing?

Did his work displease her?

Could she disapprove of his lifestyle? Was she upset that he would be leaving Manchester at the end of the exhibition?

Was she hopeful of making a match with a man of higher status and station?

Or was it something even worse?

Had she recognized his name? Had she somehow heard more damning detail about his father's criminal activity?

Was she perhaps not, as he thought and hoped, the woman that befit him most?

No. He was not certain of much, but he knew Miss Hawkins was precisely right for him. They were perfectly suited in temperament, both eager to please and to play. And the sparks that rose from every inch of his skin at her touch? Such a thing was undeniable.

Even more profound than the physical attraction, though, was the wave of tenderness, of protectiveness, and of fierce satisfaction that had come over him as they stared into each other's eyes. It had been several days since their shared moment, but not an instant passed that he did not recall the presence of her, standing before him and opening herself to him so fully.

Reflecting on the outcome of that moment—not merely the most remarkable kiss of his life but also the depth of understanding he was sure he felt for her—he shook his head in astonishment.

She was there, in his arms, in his heart, and then she walked away.

How could he have misunderstood so badly?

Martin avoided the gallery containing the painting of the two young lovers locked in that intense gaze. The piece still made him uncomfortable, but no longer for the same reason. Now that the mystery of his impression was solved—of course he felt intrusive; it was so clearly a private, intimate moment—he felt his own loss of that same cherished connection.

Was it possible Rosanna might never come here again?

Martin knew if he did nothing but move from gallery to gallery, he would run mad. He needed immediate occupation.

He turned and walked toward the room where the board members occasionally gathered. Meeting Mr. Totten at the door, Martin bowed and asked if there was any new information about Tuesday's royal visit.

"I have, of course, been in touch with the royal security detail," Mr. Totten said, nodding at his own importance.

Martin waited for more information.

Nothing.

"Very good," Martin said when nothing further was volunteered. "And?"

Mr. Totten continued to nod.

"And what do I need to be aware of?" Martin prompted.

The nod turned to a shake of the head. "All is in preparation," Totten said.

"Yes?" Martin needed a plan of action, not the verbal equivalent of a pat on the head. "And where shall I meet the entourage? What is an appropriate distance to maintain between the queen and everyone else in the building? Which path ought we take through the building? Does she wish to be seen and recognized by her subjects? Shall we devise a plan to keep other visitors from the galleries she plans to view? How does the royal security detail plan to use me?"

With each question Martin fired, Totten's smile grew

dimmer. Each nod lessened in intensity until, by the last question, Mr. Totten looked positively frightened by Martin. Not to mention the idea of Queen Victoria's visit.

"Well, I think, to be sure, we know . . ." Mr. Totten spluttered. "I believe your attendance will be a formality as much as anything." Saying even something so foolish seemed to give Totten some confidence. "You shall appear," he said, looking around the hallway in which they stood, "at the entryway as the royal party arrives."

He picked up speed as words seemed to occur to him. "You will walk behind them, keeping an appropriate distance."

Martin wondered if this idea of distance had only occurred to Mr. Totten after Martin himself had mentioned it.

"Strike an attitude of watchful protectiveness but not overbearing presence." This seemed to travel from Mr. Totten's mouth to his ear with the air of a particularly important phrase, so he repeated it. "Watchful protectiveness but not overbearing presence."

Martin managed not to roll his eyes.

"Be on hand to answer any questions and the like." Mr. Totten seemed to run out of platitudes at that point, for he reverted to simply nodding.

Martin wondered if the man knew that he had spent several minutes saying words but communicating nothing at all.

Procedural formality issued, Mr. Totten excused himself from Martin's company. "I must attend the Hollingsworth family on their tour," he said, head still bobbing up and down.

His tone suggested the Hollingsworth family had

provided some generous financial support for the exhibition. Many of the fine families from other counties who had donated money to bring the art treasures to Manchester made day trips to see their wealth at work. Mr. Totten was no doubt more qualified to guide these Hollingsworth people than to direct Martin's security endeavors.

He stepped into the tiny office where he had spent a very pleasant hour with Miss Rosanna Hawkins only a few days ago. Those intervening days felt interminable. Determined to put Rosanna out of his mind, Martin sat at the desk and pulled out a sheet of paper.

She stood just there, he thought. *Leaned against the desk just here.*

He shook his head to clear it.

Nonsense. Just because a woman had come into this office didn't mean he could not do his business here.

He wrote down the meaningless information Mr. Totten had given him, added the sparse details he could pull from his own experience, and created a plan. If Queen Victoria's escorts had already designed a pathway through the hall, very well. And if they came willing to put themselves into Martin's capable hands, he would lead them. Beginning with the ancients, he would take them on an artistic tour through time.

That would make the Michelangelo the midpoint of the tour.

Although he was unsure if any of the most modern pieces would interest the royal viewers, should they choose to continue the tour, it would give Martin a chance to explain the uncanny sense of the viewers' intrusion upon intimacy in the painting that had become his favorite, although he had stopped going to look at it. He could explain the power of the locked gaze.

The power he had experienced firsthand right here in this room.

Not that he planned to bring the Queen of England into this office, stand with his back to the door, and suggest they stare deeply into each other's eyes for several moments. But the thought made him smile as few things had in days.

How Rosanna would laugh to hear him suggest it.

Or at least she would have. Before her warmth turned frigid and she disappeared for days.

How was it possible he still had no clue what had brought on the change?

Perhaps he did not know her at all.

Martin finished scratching together his notes for Tuesday's visit and stood. He looked about the office again, noticing that the room felt much larger when he stood within it alone.

But it had seemed far warmer and lovelier when Rosanna had stood beside him.

Martin shook his head and straightened his coat. He had work to do. And if his rounds of the exhibits and galleries and hallways took him near a woman studying a painting, it would not be at all outside his professional purview to stop and discuss it with her.

Moving through the galleries, Martin did indeed see many people studying paintings, many of whom carried pencils and notebooks as they made sketches of the masterworks.

None of these people had a dozen pencils stabbed into the pile of hair at the back of their heads, though.

None looked so thoroughly transported by the images before them.

None tilted their chins at quite such an intelligent angle as Miss Hawkins did.

None of them caught his eye and shared a smile of such delight that it warmed him from the inside.

As he passed a painting of Mary Magdalene by Titian, he was struck with the thought that she appeared more ill than penitent. Martin stopped.

What if Miss Hawkins had fallen ill?

What if the strange way she had taken leave of him after their kiss was somehow the consequence of a violent ailment?

It was far more likely a reason for her staying away than that she had reevaluated her feelings for him and found him lacking.

Goodness, she could be suffering right now from a high fever while he wandered the galleries feeling sorry for himself.

Martin completed his circuit of the main passage and stepped outdoors, where he had several local officers posted. He caught the eye of a young constable and beckoned to him.

Tanner, the young officer with the ready grin, scrambled over to Martin and bowed. "Sir?"

"I need to step away from the exhibition for a short time," Martin said. "Would you mind taking over the interior post until I return?"

"Not at all, sir." Tanner's grin lit up his face.

"And could you tell me how I might find the address of a resident of the city?"

Tanner's smile dimmed a bit. "That is not so simple, sir.

Most people who live in Manchester don't own their property, so their names are not public record."

Martin cursed softly. Why had he thought it would be simple?

"Of course, sir, if the person you seek has bought a season's pass to the exhibition, their name and address would be in the record here," he said.

Martin stared.

"Begging your pardon if I speak too boldly, sir," Tanner said, looking apologetic and embarrassed.

"You're only a genius," Martin laughed. "That's all you are."

Tanner's smile spread across his face once again as Martin quickly strode back through the entry and let himself in the ticket sales room by a side door.

It only took the clerk in the ticket office a few minutes to find an address for Rosanna Hawkins, and Martin slapped him on the back and thanked him heartily. He would have taken the man out for a drink had he not been working—or in quite such a hurry.

He raced up the streets of Manchester, drawing glances from pedestrians and riders in carriages. He barely noticed them as he approached the neighborhood of Miss Hawkins's address.

Slowing to a walk was almost painful to Martin, worried as he was about Rosanna's health. He found himself breaking into a run several times, and he forced himself to move more calmly. He did not wish to create a scene. Breathing heavily, he rounded a corner and nearly collided with a woman.

He reached for her shoulders to prevent her falling, apologizing and feeling like a fool. Then he looked at her face.

"Rosanna," he said, gripping her shoulders, breathless both with exertion and surprise. "You are out walking."

She took a step back, removing herself from his clutches, a small smile tugging at her mouth.

"I am, sir. As are you, it appears."

Martin dropped his arms to his sides. "I came to see if you were ill."

Her smile slipped, and her brow crinkled in confusion.

"I very much hoped you were not, of course, but it has been several days since I have seen you at the exhibit hall."

Rosanna laughed softly. "Do you seek out all the people who miss a few days of the exhibition, Inspector?"

He stepped closer to her. "Perhaps I ought to take up that responsibility, but as of yet, I have not. Only the most important ones," he said, hoping she saw the truth behind the jest.

She did not follow his lead and close the gap between them, which gave Martin a moment of pain. But neither did she step away, which was a small victory in his mind.

"Have you been ill?" he asked.

"I am in perfectly good health, sir." Her smile seemed sincere, if not as open and bright as before.

"What has kept you away?" he asked, unable to keep the softness from his voice.

She looked into his eyes, seeming to take the measure of him.

"I have been working, sir," she said. "There are timelines I must keep."

"Of course," he said, although in truth it had never

occurred to him that Rosanna Hawkins had a job. "What is your profession?"

Clasping her hands behind her back, she jutted her chin forward. "I paint things. Decorations. For people's homes."

He pictured the kinds of ornaments his mother had collected, like flowered plates and porcelain shepherd statues. "That is lovely," he said, not because he had ever considered that someone made such things, but simply because everything seemed lovely when Rosanna was nearby.

"Where are you off to now?" he asked her.

"Are you on official inspector business?" she asked.

He laughed. "No. I really did come because I have been worried about you."

She did not answer him but continued to watch him.

He pushed at a lock of hair the breeze kept blowing into his eye.

The longer she stayed silent, the more foolish he felt. She, however, did not appear to be the least discomfited.

"Miss Hawkins," he said, wishing his voice did not sound so full of breath and of fear, "I am very glad to see you looking so well."

She looked down at the street and then back up at him. "Mr. Harrison, have you ever considered growing a beard?"

Had he heard her correctly? "Pardon?"

She touched her chin, running a finger along her jawline. "A beard. All the heroic types wear beards currently. Surely you've noticed."

What did she expect him to say? "I have noticed, yes. But I do not think a beard suits me. Besides, people would assume I had been a soldier in the Crimean, and I would hate to think I was getting credit for bravery I had not earned."

Whatever her intention in starting that strange little conversation, she appeared pleased by his response.

"I concur that a beard would not suit you. I'm happy we are in agreement." She gave a small curtsy and stepped around him. "Very nice to see you, Mr. Inspector Harrison," she said, walking down the street.

"Miss Hawkins, please," he called, knowing full well he looked like a desperate man. "Shall I see you Tuesday?"

A passing woman gave him a knowing smile. "That's right, dear," she said. "Keep trying."

Rosanna must have heard, for she turned and threw him a grin over her shoulder. "I will be there. It's not every day a girl gets to see a queen."

Martin could not deny the flood of warmth and happiness that washed through him at her words and her smile. He knew when he would see her again, and that was enough.

MANCHESTER HERALD-TRIBUNE

June 26, 1857

Art in Our Homes?

Lottie Hawkins

Many visitors to the Art Treasures Exhibition have paused with curiosity at the displays of furniture. How, they wonder, is this art? And who decides?

For those who grew up in exquisite homes, with centuries'-old drawing room seating, "art" such as masterfully crafted divans and armoires would be an everyday matter of household fact. One who sits upon artwork every day may well find magnificence in the commonplace, especially if that which is commonplace costs a fortune.

The rest of the population, making use of all available resources, can be justified in their raised eyebrows about household "art." To put it plainly, it seems ridiculous that an average person's dinner table might one day wind up in a gallery exhibit.

Most visitors are less likely to be surprised at the

inclusions of Limoges enamels and elegant, ancient tapes-
tries. When it comes to chairs and tables, many viewers
are unimpressed. This journalist suggests to these visitors
to move on. Stand before a display of armor. Consider the
romance of centuries past. Let the art viewers of the future
decide whether to honor your plates and forks. Beauty, as
they say, resides in the eye of the beholder.

CHAPTER 12

As Rosanna bid farewell to Martin on the street, she felt a lightness within and about her. It was unfortunate that he was so handsome. And charming. And uptight in his views. Her undeniable attraction to a man who could only look down on her work annoyed and distressed her.

Not that she required anyone's approval to do her work, but there was something inside her that wished for his. Certain he could never be a serious possibility for her, on account of his rigid disapproval of her career, she did, nonetheless, find his company delightful.

Delicious.

It was unfair and unlucky. Why could she not have felt such an attraction to Anton, who not only approved of her work but supported her in every step of it?

Martin Harrison was not a man of great style. He belonged in an inspector's uniform, and she could not imagine him drawing the attention of the people in a gathering. Anton was far more fashionable, more noticeable. More public.

She tried to erase Martin's image from her mind and replace it with Anton's dark hair, his dramatic black beard and moustache, his deep laugh. She attempted to replace the memory of Martin's breathless surprise at their encounter with Anton's confidence, but all she could call to mind was Anton's condescension and his sneer.

Anton's laugh had none of the sincerity of Martin's. Anton seemed to feel he was owed Rosanna's attentions, while Martin looked clobbered by good fortune when she smiled at him.

She had been so certain that she preferred confidence in a man. Why did Martin's deference and his gentleness keep coming to her thoughts?

She walked to the stationers and purchased the paints she needed to finish the work she had promised Anton. The Michelangelo was nearly finished—all four versions, but Anton would never need know that. She would deliver him the one she had promised, and she would begin her own business of sales and delivery with the other three.

This would be part of her work now—not only the production but also the sales of her reproductions. The thought gave her a shiver of pleasure; she saw in this step an enlargement of her independence. Her parents, she was sure, would be pleased as well.

As she paid for her purchase, her attention was drawn to the thick pile of creamy watercolor paper on the counter. With hardly a thought, she added two pieces to the paints she needed and paid for them. The idea of creating something new and lovely and not at all connected to Anton Greystone's demands made her smile.

The next time she walked through the exhibition, she would find a handsome watercolor to reproduce. A challenge, to be sure, for watercolor, although basic in its properties, was notorious about misbehaving. The control Rosanna enjoyed with oils, with pen and ink, and currently as she worked with tempera was nowhere to be found in a watercolor painting. The thought of chasing that elusive control excited her.

Home again, she set aside the watercolor paper. After the delivery of Anton's last piece, she would be able to paint as she pleased, to imitate the paintings she loved, not only the ones Anton felt certain he could sell.

She knew the Michelangelo reproductions would be a surefire beginning of her enhanced and increased business dealings. She felt a smile grow larger across her face at the thought. Freedom. Independence. Unlimited possibility.

Rosanna set the four nearly completed boards before her, closing her eyes to bring up the image of the original in her mind. Every aspect of the painting floated in her internal sight, and as she opened her eyes, she saw the tiny changes necessary to complete the work. The lightest touches of her brushes brought the original image to life over and over in her quiet room. She felt the flush of pleasure at seeing her job well done.

It was a nearly perfect feeling.

Only occasionally did Rosanna allow the memory of that other feeling rise to her heart. The slightly different feeling of placing the brush in a new way, of trying a distinctive technique, of achieving an unusual result. It was not about her current work at all, and such experiments had no place in her reproductions. Even so, the feeling floated inside her and tugged at her heart. This desire to create. To invent. To be an artist, not only a craftsman.

She allowed the thought to circle her, to warm her, for only a moment. Then she placed it firmly away, knowing it would not help her complete today's work.

Within a short time, her reproductions were complete, and as the last touches of paint dried, she circled each board, examining every inch with a critical eye.

Comparing her reproductions to the original in her memory, she saw nothing amiss. Only perfect matches of line, color, and tone.

Rosanna knelt before each of her replicas, a tiny brush of clear varnish in her hand. She placed her signature dab in the lower left corner, a spot unfinished and bare in the original. More than ever, an embellishment that would remain unseen.

As evening fell, Rosanna sat among her pictures, watching how the images changed with the setting sun and in the glow of candle flame and firelight. The paintings were lovely. The pride she felt in her work filled her.

A glance at the clock showed her it was nearly time for Anton to arrive.

She moved much of the clutter from the area, allowing the paintings a central place in view. Straightening up the accoutrements of her work, she organized the setting so it would appear as she wanted it to. New candles burned in small holders on the table, and she adjusted the cushions on the divan.

She settled herself in a chair, staring at two perfect, indistinguishable Michelangelo reproductions. At his knock, she rose to unbolt the door and welcomed him inside with a hand on his arm.

Anton smiled at her and placed a kiss upon her cheek. "A much better reception than I received upon my last visit," he said, managing to make his thanks sound as ungracious as a complaint.

Rather than answer a question he had not asked, Rosanna gestured to the finished pieces.

"I believe they are in every way identical," she said, although there was no need for the opening qualification. They *were* identical. Perfectly. "You may choose between them and take either one."

He stalked toward the display easels and placed his nose nearly to the boards, hands held over his chest with his elegant fingers entwined. For many long minutes he said nothing, just examined her work.

She listened for sounds of approval, watched for signs of a preference toward one or the other. He circled both boards, taking in every inch over and over.

Finally, he straightened, unclasping his hands and gesturing at the pieces.

"I shall relieve you of both," he said, nodding.

Rosanna laughed. "I have already told you I am keeping one. If the choice is too difficult, I would be happy to make the decision for you." She took a step toward the easels, arms outstretched to reach for one. "I am interested in trying my hand at selling some of my pieces."

It felt like such a simple sentence, but even as she spoke the words, she felt them drop with heavy finality into the room.

"No."

She tried for a smile, but even upon her own mouth it felt false. "Yes. I should like to give sales a try."

Another shake of his head, and Anton spoke again. "You are mine. Your product is mine. None of this is a debate. Your work belongs to me, and I dispatch it as I see fit."

What a perfectly ridiculous notion. Anton was losing his senses.

She made a sound of protest, but without waiting for an explanation or an excuse, Anton stepped between her and the paintings.

Arms raised, he made himself broad, blocking her from touching the paintings.

She put her hand on his shoulder, gently pressing him to move. She felt the tension in his body, from the wide set of his legs to the stiffness of his torso. She almost shrunk away from him in reflexive response, but she did not wish to appear nervous.

"Anton, you needn't crowd the paintings. Surely, one will suit as well as the other. They are, as I said, indistinguishable." She felt a tremble in her voice even as his shoulders grew more rigid. She hoped he would speak, that he would offer a hint of what he thought.

He said nothing, but beneath his black beard, his jaw worked back and forth as though he ground his teeth together.

She made a quick step to the side, gesturing to the painting on the right. "This one, then? I can wrap it for you." She glanced at his face, hoping for a compliant answer.

"They are both mine." His voice was a whisper, threatening and dangerous.

She shook her head, her heart thudding in her chest. "I shall be keeping one. You may choose which you'd like." She hoped her repeated, firm, gentle response would make him see reason and agree with her.

Instead, Greystone shoved her with the side of his arm, hitting hard against her ribs and thrusting her away from the easels.

He had struck her. She had stood up to him, and he hit her with the intent to wound.

Rosanna felt her breath leave her, unsure of whether the cause was shock that he should strike her or the pressure of the push. She stumbled into the wall, knocking loose a small drawing. The frame crashed onto the floor. For a moment, she could only stare at the shards of glass by her feet.

Had she imagined this? Was she now and forever a woman who had been struck by a man? She glanced back over at Anton.

He kept his back between her and the paintings, lifting first one and then the other into his arms, stacking them as if they were no more than ordinary lengths of board.

She caught her breath, feeling an ache in her arm where she had hit the wall. "What are you doing?" she asked, although the answer was obvious.

He made no reply.

"Anton, please," she said, reaching for the boards in his hands. "They must be wrapped, or the paint will be damaged."

He seemed not to hear her.

"Do not carry them this way. Please," she repeated.

He knew better than to carelessly place the paintings back-to-front. She was sure he did. Any touch of the back of one board against the paint of the other was an invitation to scratch the finish.

Her breath came rapidly, fear mounting with every second. "Stop," she said, raising her voice, hoping to draw his attention. "You will destroy the paintings."

At this, he finally turned.

The look in his dark eyes was cold. Brows lowered and jaw clenched, he whispered dangerously at her, "Back away." He gestured toward the wall he had pushed her into a moment before.

She saw the threat in his face and felt no interest in experiencing the promised result of her disobedience to his command.

Placing her hands before her, palms raised, she stepped away until her back touched the wall. Terror rushed through her, pounding with each knock of her heart.

Would he strike her again? Would he damage the paintings? She hardly knew which outcome she dreaded more.

"Where are the papers?" he asked.

She gestured beneath the table at the box full of soft cotton and large sheets of paper she used to carefully cover each piece for transport.

He swept one arm along the table, sending her tea things crashing to the floor alongside the tray holding pots of paint and tubes of pigment, small bottles of turpentine, and the pewter mug that kept her brushes.

"Please," she whispered over the clatter, "take care."

He gestured with his chin at the now-empty table. "Get out the wrappings," he demanded, his breathing loud and fast. "And if you do anything to damage these"—he gestured to the paintings in his arms—"you shall feel a full measure of my displeasure."

Damage them? Did he think she would mar her own paintings? But that would be the best way for her to protest his taking them—make them worthless. Unsellable.

Hardly aware of the steps she followed, she placed large sheets of paper upon the table and topped them with a soft cotton cloth, then she raised her hands to him for the first of the paintings.

The laugh that escaped him was free of mirth. "You shall not touch either of these again," he snarled.

Throat tight, Rosanna gasped for a full breath. "At least allow me to wrap them," she said, struggling against tears.

"Stand away," he said. "I warn you now, should your hand come near this board, my own hand shall fly."

She did not doubt.

Anton placed one of the finished boards upon the cotton, and the other he leaned against his leg.

He made to fold the cotton cloth over the painting.

"Wait," she said, more volume in her voice than she thought possible.

He started at her shout, lifting his arm as though prepared to strike her again.

She shook her head, pointing at the painting. "Place it face down," she whispered.

The growl that came from his throat sounded animal,

ferocious. Glaring at her, he breathed out a sharp sigh and turned the painting over.

"Fold the sides in first, then top and bottom." Her fright pinned her to the wall, but she would direct him in the proper way to protect her work.

As he followed her instructions, she wondered at her ability to continue to stand. She instructed his every step in wrapping and tying the first package, then the other.

With both wrapped paintings in his arms, he turned to face her again. "If you do precisely as I tell you," he snarled, his face far too close to her own, "you shall be paid for these pictures. However, should you decide to act contrary to my wishes, you may meet another of my employees soon." He cut his eyes toward the door before glaring down at her again. "This one's artistry is done with knuckle and blade. His work does not leave such a pretty impression as your own."

Rosanna had never heard such a threat, and she could not have imagined receiving one. Now that he had said the words, she felt the perfect, awful understanding. She nodded in acceptance.

"I believe you would be best served to stay inside your home for the next several days. I should hate for you to catch a chill." He leaned closer, his panting breath disturbing the curls that had come loose from her knot. "You will stay here until I have completed my next transactions," he clarified. "Someone shall watch your door, as a precaution."

He stepped away from her, holding the packaged paintings in his arms like a pair of trophies. "Ensure your own safety, Rosanna. Stay in until you hear from me."

For all the times he had called her "Bunny" and she had

wished to hear her own name, she could not have imagined he would now speak it to her with so much venom.

She stood, bolstered by the wall, until he let himself out, the click of the latch setting off a flood of tears.

Her sobs took her to the floor, and she lay beside the mess Anton had made knocking her belongings from the table, unable to calm herself or even sit up for many minutes. When at last the terror passed, she rubbed gently at the sore spot on her arm and looked around the room.

Without the Michelangelo reproductions, the room seemed darker, as if the paintings had shone with an internal light.

Attempts to stand showed her how ill equipped she was to move normally yet. Her legs trembled excessively. She crawled, arms quaking with leftover fear, to her bedroom, where she slipped her hands beneath her bed. There, solid and secure, were the other two *Madonna* replicas she had worked so hard to make. Identical copies, safe within her care.

She lay on the floor and cried tears of relief.

Her relief lasted only as long as her tears. As she dried her eyes, she resolved to take the only action available to her— she wrote a letter to the Manchester constabulary, reporting Anton Greystone's attack upon her.

She glanced over the message and felt her powerlessness. A single missive from an unimportant woman would make no waves among the police. They had far more serious crimes with which to deal.

She had one more avenue through which to approach the authorities, however. She quickly wrote another message, this one to her sister.

Dearest Lottie,

I need a favor. Please go to the constabulary and report an assault by Anton Greystone. I am fine, but I have no more details. Take the message to them as soon as possible.

I know it passes your comfort to take your responsibility as a newspaper writer and use it to report a crime for which you have no proof or witness. I ask you to do it regardless.

You have all my love, as ever.

Rosie

MANCHESTER HERALD-TRIBUNE

June 28, 1857

Art Fever Flooding Homes of the Wealthy

Lottie Hawkins

With each passing day and week of the Art Treasures Exhibition, more and more families are clamoring for a chance to own a piece of famous art. Many of the pieces in the exhibition are on loan from household collections, and with each name card placed beside a masterpiece, local families seem determined to make purchases of their own.

Local art dealers are taking advantage of the increased market for fine art, proffering their expertise in selling and buying. This reporter sought an interview with a Manchester native who runs a successful gallery, much of the work therein being on display at the ATE for the summer. The gallerist assures the *Herald-Tribune* that the buying and selling of masterpieces, while uncommon, does happen in these modern times, but offers this advice: anyone interested in making a sizeable cash outlay in exchange for a work of art ought to seek the advice of a solicitor. When pressed, the gallerist supposed that there might be an unseemly element within the city intent on taking advantage of overly trusting buyers.

Before you buy, request provenance.

This reporter would surely be horrified to discover a counterfeit masterpiece hanging on a wall during a morning visit to one of the city's nonpareil families. As you fill your home with artworks, Buyers, beware!

CHAPTER 13

MARTIN WOKE LONG before dawn. Nervous anticipation had made for a restless night, punctuated by strange dreams.

In one, a gruesome giant ant was dressed in the queen's clothing, tapping antennae across every sculpture and nodding at each painting as Martin showed her through the galleries and attempted to keep her from scratching priceless works of art.

In another, Rosanna acted as a translator for the queen, since, in a shocking twist, Her Majesty spoke only Swedish. When the whole of the main hall filled with pink salt water, causing all the religious paintings to glow, Martin leaped from his bed and dressed.

Better to wander for hours alone within the exhibition hall than lie in bed unable to shake off the strange fears of his sleeping mind.

Martin had never come to the exhibition grounds so early. The sun was not even tinting the sky blue, and he strolled the perimeter of the building in the agreeable privacy of darkness. The full circuit took him half an hour at his leisurely pace, and as he circled the building a second time, the sky began to lighten, deep blue dawn reflecting in the windows of the structure. One moment he watched a bird rise from the ledge at his approach, and the next he felt something crunch beneath his shoe.

He stepped backward, hurriedly removing his feet from whatever he had crushed beneath them. The brightening sky allowed him to see the small, scattered pieces of broken glass on the ground. He crouched to bring himself closer to the mess, then looked up for the source of the breakage.

A length of rope dangled, half inside and half outside, from a shattered square of glazed roofline, and Martin's training immediately propelled him forward. Taking off at a sprint, Martin kept his eye on the roofline, calculating which section of the exhibit hall had been breached. He thought he knew what stood beneath that part of the ceiling, but he hoped he was wrong.

He ran to the nearest door, unbolting the locking mechanism with a key he had never needed to use before, for he had never been the first person to arrive. Running through each dark gallery until he reached the hallway that accessed the area with the broken glass, Martin stopped, panting, and realized his fears had been founded.

More shattered glass lay on the floor in front of the Michelangelo *Madonna*. He looked right and left, taking in the gallery in both directions. He saw nothing unusual. No one ran past him. There was no shouting. No sound at all, in fact, and no blank spaces on the walls. His heartbeat began to slow with the evidence that nothing from this section seemed to be missing. Now Martin looked up, the lightening sky visible through the completely intact glazed panels.

No rope. No broken window.

Could he have miscalculated? Could the rope be hanging elsewhere?

He was not arrogant enough to deny the possibility of his ever being wrong, but he was certain about this. This was the very gallery he had seen only a few moments ago from outside, broken glass and trailing rope visible in the dawning light. Now, however, the roofline glinted in the bluing sky, undamaged and whole.

What had happened here?

Staring at the ceiling, he stepped backward and heard a familiar crunch. Shards of glass lay at his feet, splintered panes from the windows above, none of which appeared to be damaged. How could that be? He had seen the broken window from outside, as well as the rope that dangled over the angle of the roofline.

Were it not for the pile of sharp splinters of glass on the gallery floor, Martin might have believed the whole scenario a trick of his imagination.

He ran back outside and stopped at the place he had first noticed the glass. Now, with the rising sun, he could see more clearly. What he saw was disturbing, to say the least. No rope now hung from the roof. No broken panes appeared in the building. In fact, the pane he was sure had been damaged appeared even more pristine than the others surrounding it. And only the barest traces of glass remained on the grass, small pieces ground fine, as if by a boot heel.

Several possibilities rolled through Martin's head,

including a few surely inspired by adventure stories he had read as a child. But as any good policeman knew, the simplest explanations were most often the correct ones. The tumblers in Martin's mind worked quickly to line up what he saw with the most likely scenarios.

Somehow, in only the few moments between his initial discovery and this instant, someone had replaced the broken window panel, removed the rope, cleared out the shattered glass, and exited the premises.

Martin knew such a thing was nearly impossible. He also knew what he saw. He was not prone to exaggeration or flights of fancy.

In order to underscore a critical piece of the mystery, Martin stepped to the back of the exhibit hall, where a huge warehouse stored spare materials. Among boards, paint, and rugs, several large stacks of replacement window panels stood.

All evidence pointed to a robbery attempt, thwarted by his unexpected arrival before dawn. One thief on the roof must have seen him, used the rope to haul his partner up through the broken window before they had time to steal a painting, then fitted a replacement panel into the roofline, and run away while Martin was inside.

It smacked of nonsense. He knew he would sound like a man ranting when he told Mr. Totten and the board. But Martin understood what had happened as surely as if he had watched the entire sequence of events unfold. His ability to connect a series of seemingly unrelated events was one of the things that made him excellent at his job.

Had he not arrived at the exhibit hall as early as he had, he might have found a blank stretch of wall where the prized

Michelangelo now hung. At least, had still hung when he ran back outside. He hurried back around the building and through to the gallery he had just vacated.

The famous unfinished painting remained on the wall, each line becoming increasingly clear and visible in the sunlight.

He made his way to the front entrance, peering down each hallway and gallery, assuring himself that nothing was amiss. His cursory inspection complete, he roused the guard at the door. If his posture was any indication, he had been asleep in that chair for quite some time.

"What have you noticed today, Baker?" Martin asked the young night watchman on duty.

The guard stood from his chair, pulling at the ends of his coat and smartening up his sleeves. "Sir?"

"Did you hear strange noises? See torches?"

The guard looked at Martin, then finally stammered, "Tor-torches? Did something burn?"

"Not that I can see," Martin said. The young man would be no assistance at all. "As soon as your replacement comes, I need to see him. I presume you can stay a few minutes beyond your usual shift?"

Without waiting for Baker's answer, Martin turned on his heel, marching back up and down galleries with the benefit of locked doors and dawning sunlight. The hall would open in two hours, and he needed to reassure himself that none of the paintings had been damaged, or worse, were missing.

Half an hour later, the daytime front door guard found Martin making a brisk circuit of galleries. "Sir? You want to see me?"

"Good morning, Tanner." Martin hoped his greeting would hold true.

"Morning, sir," the constable replied, his ready smile shining on his face.

"Mr. Tanner, are you aware of the special guest we are expecting today?" Martin had no intention of playing coy, but he did not know how far the news had traveled about Queen Victoria's planned visit.

Tanner bobbed his head. "Oh, aye, sir. That'll be the queen, it will. A great honor."

Martin took the man by the arm and, even though they were alone in the hall, spoke with his head tipped near his ear. "There seems to have been an attempted break-in, Tanner. I need you to help me make sure all is secure."

Tanner's mouth rounded into an "O" shape, as did his eyes.

Martin handed Mr. Tanner a copy of the Art Treasures Exhibition program, the one each patron could purchase upon entry. Each artwork was listed by title, as well as signified by a number.

Martin said, "I'll begin at the bottom. You go from the top. When we meet, I expect a report of anything amiss."

"Very well, sir."

Martin folded open his brochure and moved from the last numbered artwork back through the catalog, checking the title of the work, the name of the artist, and the accuracy of the advertised location. He assumed it would be tedious work, but each time he verified that a piece was in its place, he felt a swelling of satisfaction.

Soon, crowds began to surge into the galleries, but Martin

carried on checking the brochure, penciling in a tick mark for every painting, drawing, print, artifact, or sculpture he could account for.

Martin realized he was enjoying this new kind of exposure to the beauties on display, and he had the thought, several times, that he would like to explore the entire exhibit this way, absorbing each piece in order, with Rosanna on his arm.

By the time he was expected to meet with the exhibition board, he and Mr. Tanner had reconnected, and each could assure the other that all was in place.

"Thank you, Tanner," Martin said. "Your help has been invaluable." He walked beside the guard until they approached the hallway where their paths would diverge.

"Sir," Tanner said, tipping his head and looking nervous, "do you think I could perhaps get a look at Her Highness today?"

Martin smiled. "I hope you can, and if there is a way to arrange it, I shall do so. Thank you again for your good work."

Tanner grinned and tipped his hat before hurrying off to his usual post.

Certain that he had already walked miles, Martin still paced from one end of each gallery to the other, glancing again and again at his pocket watch. He attempted to sit on a gallery bench, but found he could not stay still. When the appointed hour arrived, Martin stepped into the board's meeting room and found Mr. Totten striding from one wall to another.

"Ah, Harrison," Mr. Totten said, but then seemed to find

himself without more to say. He nodded and fussed with his waistcoat, making muttering sounds as he paced.

"Is all in readiness, sir?" Martin hoped it was so. Mr. Totten looked overcome by the mere idea that Queen Victoria might soon be on site.

"It is. I have a team posted at each door, ready to intercept the royal visitors and bring them this way. At which point, I shall set out through the exhibit halls with them, introducing them to each important artistic piece."

That Mr. Totten thought himself best suited to lead the tour was not so much a surprise to Martin as it was a poorly conceived idea. The man's words tended to run together when he became excited.

"Very well, sir. I intend to follow the tour and keep gawkers at bay, if that pleases you." Martin was unsure if Totten was listening as the man continued to murmur under his breath. Martin continued, "I shall make another trip 'round the main gallery and return to you soon."

Martin's idea, aside from getting himself out of Mr. Totten's way, was to see if he could intercept the queen's contingent and speak with the head of security.

As he approached the front entry, though, he saw Rosanna standing in a shaft of falling light. Her warm brown hair, pulled into its usual knot at the back of her head, its strands hanging loose and framing her face, glowed a deep honey color in the sunshine.

Martin had a glimpse, for a bare second, of what an artist might see when feeling drawn to paint someone: a vision of light and color and beauty that ought to be preserved so all the world could have the opportunity to view it. A twist in his heart reminded him that he had no talent for such things, but the wish remained.

"Miss Hawkins," he said, stepping to her side.

"Hello, Inspector," she said, her smile tense as she looked over her shoulder.

He wanted to inquire if she were well but remembered her chiding him for asking that question too often. What was a more appropriate opening query? He could think of nothing. He cast his mind about as he stared into her face, tilted in such a way as to catch the ray of sunlight and nearly rendering him distracted. He finally landed on, "Did you manage to finish all your work since we last spoke?"

She glanced behind her again and nodded.

"Are you awaiting someone?" Martin asked, hoping she would say no. What would he do if she had invited a friend, or even her sister to meet her? He had every intention of keeping her to himself today.

She gave him what appeared to be a forced smile and whispered, "The queen, of course. Has she arrived?"

Just as Martin began to shake his head, he saw the door open and a pair of smartly suited men enter, lean close to the ticket taker, and speak a few quiet words.

"I believe this is her party now," Martin whispered to Rosanna. "Do excuse me for a moment." He stepped away but turned back, unwilling to leave her. "Please do not disappear, Rosanna," he said softly.

He was rewarded with a more genuine smile than she had offered before, and he felt sure he could live on that for quite some time.

He stepped closer to the uniformed men and gave a crisp

salute. "Inspector Martin Harrison, at Her Majesty's service, gentlemen." His voice was low enough not to draw the attention of any bystanders.

"Thank you, Inspector," the nearer of the two guards said, a man with prodigious side-whiskers. "The queen wishes to experience the exhibition exactly as anyone else would, if you are amenable to such a thing."

Martin was in no position to argue, so he stood off to the side as the two uniformed men stepped back outside. They returned almost immediately, followed by a small crowd.

Martin recognized the queen, but as she did not pay him any particular attention, he was relieved to simply fall in behind the entourage. Two young children held the queen's hands, and Martin resolved to discover which of Her Majesty's nine children had accompanied their mother on this trip.

As Martin stepped to the rear of the queen's formation, he held his arm out to Rosanna. Given the strange outcomes of their last two encounters, he wasn't sure she would take it, but with a rush of warmth and relief, he felt her press her hand to his arm. She continued to take the occasional glance over her shoulder, and Martin found it charming that she felt nervous in the presence of royalty.

They walked closely enough to the royal party that they could hear the queen speaking knowledgeably to those walking with her. She mentioned the similarities of the building to the Great Exposition of London seven years past and immediately began to explain some details of the paintings before them.

Martin raised his eyebrows in question to Rosanna.

She tilted her head toward his and whispered, "Apparently she is quite an arts expert."

Martin had known Prince Albert's reputation for appreciating the fine arts, but he had not realized the queen's enjoyment went as far. Her intelligence and understanding were widely proclaimed, and he was pleased that such intellect went beyond statecraft. To enjoy pretty paintings was one thing; to hear the queen teach her children about the same? That was expertise. Martin's esteem for the queen grew as he listened to the woman's insightful commentary on the pieces they saw.

As they moved through each of the galleries, Rosanna seemed to unwind a bit more.

Martin, wanting to help her relax, pulled her closer so he could whisper to her. "Shall I tell you of the adventure we had this morning?"

She did not take her eyes off the painting before them, but he could see her mouth lift in a smile as she whispered, "I do love an adventure."

"I should never want to be a braggart, Miss Hawkins, but I believe I thwarted an attempted robbery."

She gasped and turned to him. "Surely not," she said, one hand lifted to cover her mouth in surprise.

He had felt much the same emotion that morning, but the effect was far more charming on her.

"You cannot mean I should have allowed the attempt to carry on," he said, hoping to coax a return of her smile.

She shook her head. "Of course not, sir, but what danger. Tragedy could have befallen you. Or a priceless artwork," she added, as if in afterthought. He felt the rush of pleasure at the order of her concern.

"Do you need to give this display your full attention, or shall I tell it?"

She gripped his arm. "Please," she whispered, intrigued. "Do tell."

Wishing he had a talent for spinning a tale, he gave it his best attempt. He began with the nightmares that had troubled his sleep.

"Not premonitions, I assure you," he said, "but an uneasy sleep, nonetheless. I arrived here before the dawn, determined to patrol every inch of the perimeter. We have precious visitors today, as you well know."

He pressed her hand, hoping she heard the compliment to herself within the words.

"Outside, at the rear of the exhibit hall, I stepped in a small pile of broken glass, and upon closer inspection, found quite a few pieces. My mind caught upon a dreadful thought, and I made haste to unlock a door. I knew I needed to make certain that a particular painting was still in place."

He watched with delight as her eyes widened with each word.

"In front of the Michelangelo—you know the one—I found more broken glass, but when I looked up at the windows in the ceiling, all was in place."

"How was it managed?" she gasped, as fully invested in his story as he had ever been in one of her comical tales of what had happened behind the scenes of a masterwork painting.

They continued to follow the royal entourage, and in

their pauses, Martin could hear Queen Victoria teaching her children about a painting.

"There is a closet, a kind of warehouse," Martin whispered to Rosanna, "where replacement pieces of wood, carpet, and glass are stored, for building repairs and the like."

She nodded for him to continue.

"I believe someone climbed up to the roof, smashed a window—making a terrific mess: glass outside, glass inside—and planned to make away with a priceless work of art." He felt himself puffing up with the warranted pride that came from a job well done.

"I frightened them away," he said, trying to keep his voice level. "They replaced the window and scarpered."

He waited for her response. Would she swoon? He had, after all, foiled the great robbery attempt of the summer.

Would she laugh in delight at his bravery?

He watched the color drain from her face. She looked positively ill.

"Miss Hawkins," he whispered, drawing her closer. "Rosanna, all is well. Every painting and sculpture and tiny scrap of paper is still here. All is well."

She nodded, glancing over her shoulder again, and then again.

"Come," he said, gesturing for them to follow the queen's company around the corner. "You shall see for yourself that all the priceless fragments as well as the finished paintings still hang in safety here."

The royal company was a few paces ahead, and Martin led Rosanna around a different wall so as to reach the Michelangelo before the queen did.

As Martin escorted Rosanna along the new path, her steps shuffled. He could feel her arm, pressed against his own, trembling. Surprised that his tale of intrigue and bravery had shaken her so badly, he whispered into her hair, "Nothing to fear, my darling."

My darling. How right it felt to say those words to her. He had never called a woman his darling before. He had the feeling that, forever after, Rosanna would be the only woman who ever received the endearment from him.

She said nothing in return, but he could wait. She had received a shock from his story. Perhaps she worried what might have befallen him in the course of his work. She was, after all, a woman of sparkling imagination. Someone who could dream up a silly situation for a painting must also be capable of projecting a possible tragic ending on a story of daring.

At last, they stood before the centerpiece of the exhibition. The piece that was now named after this city: *The Manchester Madonna.* They waited in relative silence for a moment, and then the royal entourage rounded the opposite corner. Martin drew Rosanna to the side, barely hearing Her Majesty's words of education and edification to the children who hung not only on her arms but upon her every word.

Martin and Rosanna stood to the left of the painting, and he felt a sweep of pride that he had managed, by luck and skill, to keep the masterpiece safe.

Rosanna ducked her head, tilting her chin to one side and then the other, never taking her eyes from the painting.

"All is well," Martin whispered to her. "As you can see, the painting is unharmed."

She looked at him then, her eyes wide and haunted. He had never seen her face so anxious, so troubled.

"There is something I must see," she said, her voice shaking with agitation. She spun away, grabbing his hand and pulling him at a run from the gallery.

He looked back for only a moment, but the queen's party did not require his protection any more than it required his expertise.

He followed Rosanna, wishing he could ask her what she needed, wishing he could simply grant her relief from her distress.

She stopped in front of a picture of a woman sitting on a stone wall, her dress light and airy against the deep green of the wooded hill behind her. It was a charming painting, and Martin could see it was well-balanced and nicely contrasted. He had learned much of art with this assignment, after all.

Before he could speak the thoughts in his mind, though, Rosanna performed a repeat of her duck-and-tilt observation of the painting, gasped, and ran off again, pausing only to grasp his hand in hers.

They sped off again, passing patrons and board members and security staff at every turn.

Rosanna skidded to a halt in front of a landscape piece. Once again, she bent low, tilted her head, and finally met Martin's eye.

He smiled at her, hoping his supportive presence would be sufficient for her to let go of whatever concern she felt.

"Inspector—" she whispered.

"Martin," he corrected gently, pressing her hand between his own.

"Martin," she repeated. "You've been robbed."

CHAPTER 14

ROSANNA'S STOMACH CHURNED, and the sick feeling washing over her made the fear and pain she had suffered since Anton's last, violent visit seem minuscule. Nearly forgotten were the flutters of dread upon leaving her rooms this morning, sneaking out of Mrs. Whitmore's house for the walk to the exhibition. Had she really watched over her shoulder, worried that Anton had sent one of his henchmen to watch her?

To follow her?

To hurt her?

Now that she understood Anton's intent, her fears seemed unfounded. Why worry about a silly girl, whose only skill was to copy pretty pictures, when he had a far more elegant plan in play?

She looked up at Inspector Martin Harrison's face, all concern and confusion.

"How," he asked, his voice shaking, "do you know we've been robbed?"

How to explain?

How to convince him?

Every negative impression, every ounce of contempt he carried about reproduction painters would be compounded in his mind if she told him, without reservation, that her paintings had been switched into the exhibition galleries. Each tender moment she and Martin had shared would be rubbed away by his response to her work, the same response she resented only yesterday, but now had to admit held some merit.

She was a forger. Unwilling, admittedly. But her unwitting assistance had made it possible for Anton—for who else could it be?—to steal some of the greatest works of art in European history.

If she had known what Anton Greystone would do with her paintings, she would never have given him her work. This was appalling, in exactly the way Martin Harrison had pictured it. But she was not entirely guilty. She had not agreed to this. She was in no way complicit in the horrible deed; no one could imagine her to be so. She could not have invented Greystone's scheme, but regardless of her intentions, her paintings were now hanging on the walls of the Art Treasures Exhibition, replacing priceless masterpieces.

How could she explain the truth to Martin without sounding like she was in on the plot? What could she say to express her utter surprise at this outcome?

She decided the fewest words would likely bring the best understanding.

She pointed at the painting hanging on the wall before them. "I know because I painted this."

He shook his head as if to clear away a fog. "I do not understand."

"This is my work," she said, "and I can prove it." Knowing how he felt about reproductions, she forced herself to be perfectly clear. "Recreating masterpieces is what I do for my employment. Each of my reproduced paintings bears my mark—including this one. And *The Manchester Madonna.*"

There. Now, surely, he would understand and offer consolation for the way in which she had been ill-used. She stepped forward, eager for the safe comfort of his arms around her in this moment of horror and perplexity.

She ducked into his chest, awaiting the warm embrace.

Instead, she felt one of his arms, steely strong rather than gentle, turn her and grasp both her wrists behind her back.

"Miss Hawkins, you are under arrest," he said.

His voice, which she knew could move in the mildest of tones from his lips to her ears, sounded completely foreign to her.

"Pardon?" she asked.

A mirthless laugh escaped his mouth. She looked up to see his jaws clamped tight.

"I shall grant you no pardon," he said, in the same cutting, heartless voice.

She stumbled as he propelled her forward, and he used his other hand to steady her elbow. There was no tenderness in this touch, only efficiency.

From one step behind her, he directed her down one gallery and another, turning corner after corner until they reached the same small office where they had—

She could scarcely think of that now. They entered the

room, and she waited to hear him explain his actions. To make sense of what he had said. To justify the following silence. She turned to face him.

Without another word, with barely a glance, Martin spun on his heel and exited the small office, closing the door with a finality that took the strength from her knees. She sat in the uncomfortable wooden chair and heard a snicking sound of the door locking.

Was this actually happening?

When Martin had told her of the foiled break-in, she could not shake the fear that he was mistaken, that the attempted robbery had not so easily been frustrated. She worried the intruders were far more sophisticated than Martin imagined.

And she was correct.

She knew it now.

Martin had guessed accurately at certain pieces of the puzzle, she was sure. Someone had broken through the ceiling, had let a partner down a rope, and had replaced a glazed panel of the windowed ceiling.

What Martin had not understood was the true cost of the disturbance. As he had run from outside to inside, someone else had done the same but in reverse. While Martin sighed in relief to see Michelangelo's masterpiece still hanging upon the wall, the original was being carried out of the exhibit hall, along with at least one Gainsborough and a Cole.

Tragedy enough, certainly, but Rosanna sagged as she realized there could be dozens more. She had created so many reproductions. Had Mrs. Ellsworth and her like purchased them all? Or had Anton held on to them, anticipating a chance such as this?

At the very moment Martin ran through and checked that every piece was in place, the true artworks were removed under cover of predawn darkness. He had mistaken her reproductions for originals throughout the exhibition halls. Rosanna knew the truth as clearly as if she had seen it unfold before her eyes.

How could she have been such a fool?

Trusting Anton Greystone was the greatest mistake of her life. She had believed his claims that all was lawful and just, even when he seemed at times to be otherwise. She believed him because she'd wanted to believe him.

She had been to Mrs. Ellsworth's salon and had been introduced as the genius behind the parlor reproduction. So, as far as Rosanna knew, Anton's stories of other buyers, other parlors, and other collectors were true.

And curse it all, she was good at this. She had incredible talent. Her gift lay in seeing and reproducing flawlessly the works of the masters. If only her skill had been to see Anton's character more clearly.

She knew Anton Greystone. Knew from experience in those same salons his ability to turn a conversation to his benefit. Knew his skill at stroking a person into confident complacency. Knew his penchant to sweet-talk a buyer with a well-placed compliment.

All of these made him an excellent salesman.

And a practiced liar. And yet, she had believed him.

Rosanna looked around the spartan office, bare of anything connecting it to Inspector Harrison. Nothing of his personality resided here. She spotted a small book on the desk: the exhibition program that sold for a few pennies. Flipping through the pamphlet's pages, she saw tiny, perfect tick marks showing where he had noted the paintings were hanging where they should be. He'd made these marks only this morning.

This morning, when he felt secure, when the world was filled with honest people.

This morning, before he arrested her.

This morning, when he still loved her.

She could see it now, that tender look in his eyes, could feel the press of his hand around hers. How gentle he was, how kind and sincere. Each memory of his affection, from a smile and a laugh to the powerful and tender touch of his lips against hers, flooded her with regret. She had never held him in such high esteem as she did in this moment, when she knew he never would smile at her again.

He thought she was a criminal.

And he was correct.

She *was* a criminal. A forger. An unwitting accomplice to a horrific act of thievery, but an accomplice nonetheless.

Rosanna folded her arms upon the small wooden desk, lay down her head, and sobbed.

CHAPTER 15

MARTIN PULLED THE KEY from the lock and stood with his back against his office door, sick and stricken.

How could he have misjudged Rosanna so completely? He thought she was sweet. He thought she was charming. He thought she was delightful, but it was all part of her criminal act.

Naturally she would need to hone these skills in order to pull off such reprehensible and deceitful activities as forgery and theft.

Martin shook his head, disgusted with her. And with himself.

Shouldn't he have been able to see through her act?

Ought he not to have noticed the ill-intent lurking behind the sweet smile? Of course he ought. Not only was he trained to look beyond the surface, but he had years of practice seeing through lies and deception. Every thug, ruffian, and jackanapes, each cutpurse and pickpocket worth his wicked reputation, had a way of winkling his way out of trouble for his misdeeds.

Martin could see through a mustache-twisting criminal before he could count to three. How could he have mistaken Rosanna Hawkins so completely? She was a charlatan. A fraud. A counterfeiter.

He had stood behind her and watched her work, seen the way she imitated the lines of famous artists' work. With her obvious talent, how could he not have known?

But he had never been able to see it in his father either. During all his childhood years, he believed his father was a shopkeeper. After all, away he went to the shop every morning, and back he came every evening. Martin visited the shop himself, as a lad, to see the wonderful things his father sold.

The shop was a treasure trove. Everything a child could think to look for was on display and for sale in Martin Harrison Senior's emporium—tin soldiers, toy trains, games, swords from a century of wars, antique battle gear—not to mention the rows and shelves of things Martin never even bothered to notice like delicate tables, chandeliers, rings, cravats, watches on chains or off, heavy vases, framed pictures, and rows and rows of books on shelves.

His father even had friends who were constables, predecessors of the Bobbies and Peelers, who came and went from the Harrison home.

But Martin was blindsided by the truth when he learned that what his father sold was not, in fact, his to sell. "A dealer in stolen artifacts"—that was what the courts officially called his father. Those whose watches, jewelry, cutlery, horse tack, and other stolen goods he sold were more likely to use different words.

Thief. Confidence man. Scoundrel. Bandit. Brigand. Highwayman.

Each of those remembered words rained down shame on Martin's head. With every thought of his father's depravity, Martin stood taller in his confidence and pride that he'd chosen the opposite path. His police training, his work in the London constabulary, his ascent to the office of inspector all showed him, every day, that he had risen above his father's name.

He knew the difference between lawfulness and lawlessness. He could discern a decent person from a swindler.

Or so he had thought. Until today.

How wrong he had been. How easily a turned-up face with a charming smile had fooled him into ignoring his duty and overlooking the danger of deception.

Never again, he promised himself. Never again would he allow such fraudulence to trick him.

And now he needed to pull himself away from this locked door and do his job.

He took a deep breath and headed deeper into the exhibition, where he knew Mr. Totten was still touring with Queen Victoria's entourage. Darting from hall to gallery, Martin caught up with the group as the queen made her way slowly around a sculpture, pointing out to her children how the artist managed to make stone appear light and airy.

Martin stepped beside Mr. Totten. "Sir, if I may have a moment of your time."

Totten shook his head. "After the royal visit has concluded," he muttered. "As the head of the committee, I must remain close to our distinguished guest." He practically bowed, even though the queen was enraptured by the statue on the plinth.

"But, sir," Martin insisted, "I am afraid there is a problem."

With a blustering breath, Totten turned to face him, blame clouding his features. "Has your security team failed us? Today of all days?" It was more an indictment than a question.

Martin shook his head, even though he was fairly sure the answer was yes. "The team is in place, sir. All entrances and exits are secure."

"Are we—that is, the royal family—in danger?" he asked, his head swiveling as if whatever threat had appeared would step into the gallery at any moment.

"No, sir. Not that kind of problem."

With careful enunciation, slowly and with a hint of menace, Mr. Totten said, "Then, Mr. Harrison, it is your problem to solve. That is, after all, what we employed you to do." He turned his back on Martin and stepped away.

Martin kept his reply to himself and made his way out of the gallery.

What to do?

Something was stolen; he must get it back.

Rosanna Hawkins was involved.

Pushing through a small gathering of people, he mumbled pardons and marched back toward the locked office where she waited.

After a few steps, it occurred to him that the only reason he knew the theft had occurred at all was because she told him it had.

He believed her without a second thought. Why, he wondered, had she said anything?

Did her guilt manifest itself so readily?

That didn't say much for her success in a criminal lifestyle. She'd not last long if she immediately confessed to her crimes.

He shook his head.

Rosanna—Miss Hawkins, that is—might have been protecting someone. A partner. Someone on the outside.

And now his only source of information was locked in his office. Giving the partner time to move the stolen property.

Blast, he thought. There was no more time to waste.

He needed to gather enough information in order to move forward and recover the stolen pieces.

He reached the locked door and turned the key. As he pushed the door open, Rosanna Hawkins raised her head from her arms and looked at him with a face full of regret. Eyes streaming, she stood from the chair she had been sitting in.

"Martin," she said, tears in her voice.

"You may call me Inspector Harrison, and you may speak in answer to my questions." His voice, firmer than he expected, seemed to shock her.

She sat back down.

"Who is your accomplice?" he demanded.

She shook her head. "I beg your pardon?"

"Your partner. Your co-conspirator?" he said. "Come now, Miss Hawkins. We do not have time for either of us to play the fool."

She wiped the tears from her face. "I have no intention

of playing the fool, or of playing at all," she said, firmness returning to her voice. "But I need to state my innocence."

He scoffed.

The sound seemed to deflate her, but she continued speaking. "I do have a business partner, and it is possible that he has replaced some of the paintings in this exhibit with my reproductions. But if you are convinced that I have somehow masterminded a theft, you are sorely mistaken."

She paused for a shuddering breath. He remained silent.

"If that is the case, *Inspector*," she said, laying heavy emphasis on his title, "I have very little information that will be useful to you."

"That is not a conclusion for you to draw," Martin said. "I will determine how useful your information may be."

Her eyes narrowed, but she said nothing.

He stood before her. "Miss Hawkins, what is the full name of your accomplice?"

She started to protest, but he held up his hand between them. "Time is essential here. If you please, simply answer the question."

"My *employer's* name is Anton Greystone."

"His address?"

She shook her head. "I do not know where he lives, nor do I have an address of his place of business."

He shifted his weight and forced his voice to be calm. "Do you expect me to believe you do not know where your"—he cleared his throat—"*partner* lives and works?"

He watched a blush rise in her face, and he felt both ashamed and gratified that his tone conveyed his disbelief.

She managed to still meet his eye. "You may choose to

believe or disbelieve as you wish. I have told you the truth." The way she squeezed her hands together belied her calm voice.

The fact that she was correct did nothing to dissuade his line of questioning.

"Where, then, did the two of you conduct your business?" he asked.

"In my rooms," she responded. Was that a challenge in her gaze?

Her rooms. Which rooms, precisely? Her home? Alone? The two of them? He wondered but dared not ask. Martin felt his own face coloring. He hoped she did not notice.

She noticed. "I am a grown, independent woman, Inspector, and my experience and intellect combine to allow me free use of my judgment to determine who may visit my home."

He knew his thoughts were written on his face. He shook his head, wishing she would stop looking at him like that.

Again, she seemed to read his mind. "Is my virtue being called into question, sir? Because I rather thought you were in a hurry."

He looked at the table and then forced his eyes to meet hers. "Does your partner keep a warehouse? A storage facility?"

"I believe you would do better to simply ask me what I think he might be doing with the stolen paintings."

Martin sputtered. "I *am* asking you that. But there are protocols."

She sighed and waited for him to speak.

"Yes, well . . ." He cleared his throat and began to pace

the small room. "Then. In that case, what do you think he has done with the paintings?"

The lines around her mouth softened. Not into a smile, but away from the rigidity of a moment ago.

"He can't keep them. People talk. You and I are the only people, outside of his associates, who are currently aware the paintings have been switched. I, because I painted them. You, because I told you. Anton and his men know because the paintings passed through each of their hands. But once word gets out that he has valuable artwork to sell, he will not be able to keep the information secret. And he will not be able to hold on to the pieces. He will try to off-load the paintings."

She reached behind her in what appeared to be an unconscious movement and pulled a pencil from her hair. She tapped it on the table before her as she spoke.

"He has several buyers here in Manchester," she mused. "You ought to send a Peeler to speak with Mrs. Ellsworth in Cheetham Hill. She has purchased many of my reproductions this summer, and I believe Anton has promised her my version of the Michelangelo."

Writing notes in his small leather-bound notebook, Martin stopped and looked up at her. "This partner of yours would hang an irreplaceable, priceless artwork in the salon of an amateur collector?" He could hear his voice rising in indignation and disbelief.

The corner of her lip raised a nearly imperceptible degree. Only someone as used as Martin was to gazing at her mouth would even have noticed.

"I believe, sir, it was only a week since that you offered quite a different opinion about the worth of that particular piece." Miss Hawkins's speech remained even, which infuriated him. How could she be so calm?

"Need I remind you that you are under arrest?" Martin asked, regretting the words as soon as they were spoken.

Her reply was quick and short. "You need not." She tapped the table again.

"So, if I may restate your testimony, you think that . . . Mr. Greystone, was it? That he has delivered the painting to Mrs. Ellsworth of Cheetham Hill?" He checked his notations before looking at her.

"No."

"No? Miss Hawkins, then why did you tell me that?" Insufferable woman.

"If you would care to review your careful transcription of our conversation, I simply suggested you send someone to speak with her. Give her a warning that her art dealer might be involved in something unsavory." She shifted in the wooden chair. "I believe you need to check the railway."

He was baffled. "The railway." He repeated her words, not as a question but simply to have something to say.

"Inspector, Mr. Greystone must get the paintings as far from himself as possible. Of course, in order to allay suspicion, he could unload them in the least likely places, such as in my rooms—where, I assure you, the originals are not—or in the home of one of his buyers. But it is far more likely that he will simply get on a train and leave the city."

"To London?"

She shook her head. "I doubt it. We can presume there is not a more famous artwork in the kingdom at this moment than this Michelangelo. Every newspaper has carried stories of its newfound provenance. If word gets out that *The Manchester Madonna* has been taken, all of England will turn its eyes toward London. No, if I know Anton, he will send the pieces to the Continent. After which time, Inspector, they will be far out of your reach."

Martin knew the reputations of criminal networks operating all over Europe. The trading, selling, buying, and hiding of stolen goods had a long and fascinating history, a history he was uncomfortably familiar with, thanks to his father's unsavory business dealings. But how much did Miss Hawkins truly understand? How deeply was she involved in this madness?

"To Liverpool?" he asked, quietly dreading her answer.

"To Liverpool," she replied with a single nod of her head.

CHAPTER 16

ROSANNA WATCHED Inspector Harrison step out of the small office, and as she heard the lock click once again, she wondered if she would be imprisoned in this room all day. All night. Until someone either found Anton or gave up the chase.

She stood from the chair and walked the perimeter of the office. As far as distance covered, it was unimpressive, but she felt better in motion.

Had he believed her?

He certainly did not seem to, at least at first. Inspector Harrison was ready, willing, and eager to find her guilty of the theft of the masterworks.

In fact, he likely already had laid the blame at her feet, without allowing the kind of doubt that might make him think twice, that might make him consider what he knew of Rosanna, of her heart.

She knew uncovering culpability and blame was a central aspect of his work. So dreadful, so dark an outlook. She knew that one saw what one looked for—whether that was beauty or roughness—and she could not imagine living a life where guilt was one's focus. It must be exhausting for him, she supposed, to be constantly on the lookout for such vices.

It was almost forgivable. Even in her innocence, she simmered with frustration for the sake of her own good name. Yes, Martin Harrison's work must be exhausting both physically and mentally, but it was also infuriating. She could pity but not pardon, for how could someone be forgiven for seeing guilt that was simply not there?

Insufferable man. Could he not see in her face that she had known nothing of the planned theft? He knew her well enough to see her innocence, her horror, and her devastation about the paintings. At least, she corrected herself, he should have.

She mentally counted all the reproductions she had made since the exhibition opened in May. Dozens of paintings, perfect facsimiles. Was even more of her work here on display? Could Anton have replaced every original with her work?

She was certain only of the Cole, the Gainsborough, and, most importantly, the Michelangelo. Those all bore her secret mark. She had to get out of this room and discover how many other paintings she had reproduced were replaced.

She alone could be certain of how many originals Anton had absconded with. How many hours had passed since the theft?

She walked to the tiny room's door, knocked, and called out, "Hello? Is there someone who can hear me? Hello?"

Had she received an answer, she was not certain what she might say, for as gifted as she was in the mimicry of paintings, she had very little talent for telling outright lies.

I seem to have locked myself in this room from the outside?

It appears that in quest of a painting by Reubens, I accidentally found myself in a hallway filled with office space and decided to explore the artless walls?

No. It was unlikely she could offer an excuse believable enough to convince anyone to help her escape her makeshift prison cell.

When nobody answered her calls, she sighed in both relief and frustration.

In the absence of a guard at the door, she must make do as she could.

She gripped the doorknob, but it did little more than rattle under her hand. Pulling a single pin from the collection holding her curls at bay, she straightened it and inserted one end into the locking mechanism.

She had some experience unlocking doors from her childhood exploits when she would free her sisters and herself from their nursery to spy on guests at their parents' dinner parties. Nursery doors were surely less complicated than a door like this. She was unprepared for the lock to spring so quickly and for the door to open. With barely a thought, she stood in the doorway, unfettered and unrestricted. A quick glance down each side of the hallway showed her that she was completely alone.

Walking with resolve, she made her way toward the galleries. At the first corner, she paused to take a steeling breath and then turned toward the crowds.

If there were three thousand people at the exhibition today, there was a one in three thousand chance she would encounter Inspector Harrison. Would her likelihood increase if she hoped not to see him?

Or was he gone? Had he left the premises to search for the missing paintings?

Would he search her home first and find her hidden reproductions? He knew where she lived, as evidenced by his arrival outside Mrs. Whitmore's boardinghouse only days ago. She had not questioned how he had found her, but perhaps he knew far more about her than she had previously supposed.

And, at the same time, he knew nothing about her at all.

With that thought, her anger flared again. How dare he accuse her of taking part in this dreadful pursuit? Anyone who knew her heart knew she had only the purest motives.

Or so she had always thought. Were her intentions perhaps more mercenary than wholesome? Was being paid to recreate masterworks as base a crime as Inspector Harrison made it sound?

Unwilling to peel away the layers of ethical murkiness clouding her heart and her work, she continued to walk through the mingling crowds toward the exit doors, her back straight and her head high.

At a gallery of Titian pieces, she caught the eye of one of Queen Victoria's guards, who nodded in recognition from earlier in the afternoon.

Her breath hitched, and she froze. Letting her eyes travel casually over the gallery, she took in the assembled entourage, nodded back to the man, then stood for a moment as if studying a painting on the opposite wall and waited for her heart to resume beating.

When the guard withdrew his glance without any show of surprise or concern, she let out a long, silent exhale.

Her blood rushed through her, tingling the skin from the back of her neck to her forearms, raising tiny hairs. Panic. Or was it pleasure? How odd the similarity of sensations.

But before she stepped away from the gallery, she paused. When, if ever, would she again stand in such close proximity to royalty?

She took in the way the queen bent her head toward her daughter, speaking in a low voice and sharing a grin about some mutual delight.

Rosanna's heart captured the memory, and she hoped she might have a chance to set this moment down on paper or canvas. Possibly even present a portrait as a gift to the queen. Might she step a bit closer to hear what the queen said about the painting she studied? Might she herself be called upon to offer an opinion?

All too soon, reality swept away such thoughts. She had no time to waste hoping for a royal encounter. With measured steps, she strode away from Queen Victoria and her royal entourage, hoping to remain invisible as she made her way to the exit.

Thirty more steps. Twenty. Ten. She felt her heart pound in time with her feet.

At the exit door, she exhaled her held breath, squinting into the grayish brightness of an overcast sky. She had made it. Without incident and without the slightest confrontation.

Now, to find proof of her innocence.

A hand closed around her upper arm. This time the flush of energy through her body had no essence of pleasure. Fear hurtled through her, centered in the pressure of the man's fingers on her arm.

"Miss," said a young man wearing the jacket of the exhibition's security detail, a weary expression on his face.

Rosanna took it in instantly. Poor man, tasked to wait for her to emerge from the exhibition hall, dreading his duty. He now had to apprehend her. How distasteful to a person like this: a young man of sweet temper, if his face and posture told her true. She wondered if she could pull away from him and make a getaway, rendering his disagreeable duty unnecessary.

"Miss," he repeated, "I been calling you, miss. You must not have heard me."

She said nothing, attempting to steady her breathing.

"You dropped this, miss," he said, holding out a pencil that must have fallen from the collection she maintained in her hair.

She stared at him, open-mouthed.

"Miss, this is yours, I believe," he said, this time with a slower cadence, as if she did not understand English, or perhaps needed to read the words on his lips. He held the pencil on his upraised palm, a gesture of deference in the slight bow of his head.

"Indeed, I thank you," Rosanna said, the words emerging in a husky whisper. Heart thudding, lungs squeezed, she took the pencil from his hand and turned and fled, feet pounding along the graveled path, pulling in ragged gasps of air and allowing the incoming crowds to bump past her.

As she ran down the lane, past the hundreds of people making their way toward the exhibition hall and its treasures, she hoped her hasty retreat would go unremarked. The longer she could remain anonymous, the better chance she had of staying ahead of Inspector Harrison.

Eyes straight ahead, she told herself. One foot after the other. She moved through the crowds, through the throng. Away. Away.

Once out of the park where the exhibition hall stood, she felt far more confident at her ability to blend in with the people streaming through the streets of Manchester, entering shops and going about their business. She slowed to a quick walk, matching her steps to the other people on the street, and with a turning here and there at each intersection, made her way toward home.

Mrs. Whitmore sat in the front parlor of her boarding-house, a needle and linen cloth in her hands.

"Miss Hawkins," she said with her customary nod.

"Hello, Mrs. Whitmore," Rosanna said, feet already on the staircase. "Has anyone come for me recently?" She attempted to add a lightness to her tone, but she knew she sounded breathless.

Mrs. Whitmore tilted her head as she stabbed her needle into the cloth. "A gentleman was here, but as I didn't recognize him, I told him he may attempt a call again tomorrow. I haven't seen your young man for a few days," she added with a knowing look. As usual, her tone invited but did not demand Rosanna's confidence.

She wondered at the best way to respond.

She decided on a partial admission. "Mr. Greystone will not be welcome back here," Rosanna said, gripping the ban-ister.

She caught Mrs. Whitmore's understanding nod, and then hurried to her rooms.

Unlocking the door, entering, and locking it again behind her, Rosanna ran through her rooms, making a cursory inspection. Nothing seemed any more disturbed than the slightly disheveled way she left it.

Falling to her knees beside her bed, she slipped the two remaining duplicates of Michelangelo's painting out from their hiding place. Grateful that she had taken the time to wrap them carefully before she had stored them away, she now lifted both into her arms, inspecting the twine that secured the wrapping. The strand of hair she had entwined with the string and knotted around the packages was unbroken, reassuring her that no one had meddled with it.

Laden with the packages, she let herself out of her rooms once again, locking the door behind her. She wondered if this might be the last time she would be allowed to close that door behind her. Perhaps someone else would soon be locking the door of her next lodging—with her secured inside.

Try as she might to keep her thoughts positive, the idea would not leave her mind. Prison. Good heavens, prison. She'd been detained by a police inspector. Arrested. Like a common criminal. Not to mention she had *escaped*.

She thought of her family. Her poor father had always been the staunchest supporter of his daughters, proudly saying to anyone who would listen that these girls of his would show the world what educated women could do. She doubted that "wind up in prison" ever entered his imagination.

And her mother. Bless her, Elizabeth wanted nothing more for her family than happiness. Happiness in their studies, their work, their relationships. Rosanna's heart tugged at the thought of how this might end for her dear mother.

Would Lottie write the newspaper article that documented Rosanna's prison sentence? Perhaps Ella might stand on the road at the side of the prison, playing plaintive melodies on her violin as a message of love and support.

Shaking her head, Rosanna refocused on the most pressing issue at hand.

She had to find the missing paintings. But what if they had truly disappeared? If she were unsuccessful at locating Anton and the original paintings, only Rosanna would be left to suffer the consequences of Anton Greystone's nefarious actions.

She made her way down the stairs and into Mrs. Whitmore's parlor. She bent to kiss her housemistress on the cheek, a sign of affection often felt but only occasionally shown.

"And what is that for?" the good woman asked, tucking away her stitchery and grinning broadly.

Rosanna tried for a cheery laugh. "It is in thanks for your kindness, of course. And we both know you deserve much more," she said, feeling a prickle at the corners of her eyes.

What if she never returned here? What if this was her goodbye to Mrs. Whitmore?

"Will you be joining me for tea?" Mrs. Whitmore asked.

"I think not today," Rosanna answered. She was certain she would not make it back by teatime.

She could very well be in prison by teatime.

However real the possibility, it did not do to dwell upon

it. She stepped once again into the gray light of the afternoon and turned her feet toward the rail station.

Carefully gripping the wrapped paintings by the edges, Rosanna marched through the busy streets with her head held high but felt the fear mingling with her growing uncertainty. Could she find Anton in the crowded city? Was she too late? Could she somehow put right this tremendous wrong?

Try as she might to convince herself that she was free of any blame, a seed of doubt grew in her mind. Had she perhaps crossed a line in her work? Was she guilty of aiding a criminal? Martin—Inspector Harrison—had no doubt about her full complicity in Anton's plans.

She had not succeeded in convincing the inspector that she was an innocent bystander, caught unawares in Greystone's web of deception. And now that she thought of it, how could the inspector think otherwise?

Naturally, if there was a simple explanation, it was likely the rational one, and the simple explanation was that Rosanna painted copies so Anton could pass them off as originals and steal away with the true masterpieces.

Oh, dear, she thought.

How could she have overestimated Anton? How had he deceived her so completely? How foolish she was to trust his motives even when she knew his capacity for anger, and now for violence.

She pushed past a knot of people looking in a shop window, clutching the wrapped paintings closer to her and clenching her teeth together.

Even thinking of Anton brought every repulsive feeling to her heart. She thought of the way he pandered to her, how he gave her compliments that she could not believe, his often weeks-long inattention was followed with drippy, patronizing insincerity. How her skin had crawled lately at his touch.

She tried hard to ignore her memories of earlier times, when his kiss—as well as his words—had been far more welcome.

But she forgave herself some of those responses; she had been young then.

The thought was small comfort; she was young *now*. But some measure of innocence inside her was lost forever. Lost at the hands of a man in whom she had placed her trust, her talents, her finances, and her future.

Was she making a similar mistake now? Giving her confidence too freely? Was she retreading the same steps of false security with Inspector Harrison?

Could any man truly be trusted?

The facts seemed to point to *no*. But the truth of Martin's affection pushed past the cold facts, and she hoped—oh, how she hoped—that the truth would prevail.

Perhaps only time, heartbreak, and further misconceptions would tell.

$\mathcal{C}$HAPTER 17

MARTIN, STRUGGLING UNDER the weight of discouragement he felt by being, once again, deceived by someone he trusted, made his way from the exhibition to the Manchester constabulary.

Upon presenting his credentials to a young man at the small table in the entrance vestibule, he impatiently awaited an audience with Edward Collier, head of the Manchester office.

He found himself tapping his feet on the floor and remembering how Rosanna tapped her pencil upon the table, an affectation that was possibly unconscious or possibly practiced. Either way, it was enchanting.

How many moments had he spent thinking of the tilt of her head, of the pile of pencils in her hair? He had filled most of his waking hours considering her face, her hands, her movement, her smile. She was utterly captivating.

Captivating, and now captured.

He had gone from kissing her to arresting her, which was

not, in any of his daydreams, the way he'd hoped his relationship with Miss Hawkins would have played out.

He'd never once considered locking her away in his office to prevent her stealing a stack of famous paintings.

He almost laughed at the thought.

But the idea was less funny and more horrible, and he stared down the hallway, willing Collier to appear.

Finally, the man approached, his graying ginger hair combed back from the peak of his forehead, side-whiskers partly concealing his somewhat pointy ears. Martin had the fleeting feeling he was speaking to a fox in the process of becoming human.

Collier stopped in front of Martin and held his hands behind his back, at his ease in his own constabulary.

"I am Inspector Martin Harrison," Martin said, introducing himself directly.

"Martin Harrison?" The policeman did a double take, then squinted as though looking for something familiar in Martin's face.

"Currently head of security at the Art Treasures Exhibition," he said, hoping to derail the questions he knew were coming.

"Right, but Martin Harrison? The fence? Arrested, what, fifteen years ago? Hang on. Stay right here." He stepped away and called down the hall. "Wiggins—get over here. Someone you need to see."

Wiggins.

The arresting officer who had put his father away. The man who had written to Martin at least once each year to encourage him to take advantage of his opportunities, to seek a position with the Peelers, to turn his life to justice and protection instead of following his father's footsteps.

A thin, stooped man followed Collier around the corner.

"Look at this," Collier said, gesturing to Martin. "It's like his very ghost has come to see you again, innit?" He gave the thin man a jostling pat on the shoulder, and Martin worried the older man would fall over.

"You're Martin Junior?" Wiggins asked, but nodding already, his face a picture of understanding. "Robert Wiggins," he said, gesturing at himself. "I'm he what caught your father."

"I know, sir." Martin wished Collier would disappear for a moment, or for an hour. There were things he would like to say to Wiggins in private. Things he would like to ask.

Wiggins nodded, and a warm smile spread over his face. "It has been a great many years since I have seen you. And what a fine gentleman you have become."

Martin had a strong urge to run into the man's arms and allow himself to be hugged. Instead, he held out his hand. "I thank you, sir, for your correspondence and your support."

Mr. Wiggins wrapped Martin's hand in both of his own. "You do us all proud, son," he said in a whisper, his words landing directly in the space that Martin's absent father had left, that space which would always crave such statements.

Collier watched the two of them.

"Did you come to see me, Inspector Harrison?" Wiggins asked, darting a glance at Martin's uniform. The mention of his title came with another warm smile.

"Not specifically, but maybe you can help. It has only just come to my attention that several masterpieces have been stolen from the exhibition. Stolen and replaced with near-perfect replicas."

Martin watched Collier and Wiggins for responses. Wiggins held Martin's gaze and nodded in understanding. Collier began bouncing upon his toes, as though Martin had told him the most thrilling tale he'd ever heard.

"I'm headed to the railway—to Liverpool—to try to apprehend the paintings and the perpetrator," Martin continued, "but I came to ask if your office could see its way to sending an officer or two to the Ellsworth family in Cheetham Hill. Mrs. Ellsworth is a collector who has previously done business with the man we suspect of the theft. I assume the Ellsworths are unaware of the illegal activities at hand, but I would appreciate your assistance in discovering anything she may know about a man calling himself Anton Greystone."

"Delicious." Collier laughed, a short bark, and rubbed his hands together. "Wonder if that is truly what he is called. Sounds like a name Mr. Dickens would give a villain."

Martin, feeling the pressure of passing time, turned from Collier to Wiggins. "I would be grateful for any help."

Wiggins gave his attention to Collier. "Sir, I will gladly take a junior officer and interview Mrs. Ellsworth if you agree."

Collier, still smiling, bobbed his head. "Of course, of course," he said. "Drive yourself out there to the great blooming manors and see what you can discover that will help our young friend here." Collier leaned closer to Martin and tapped the side of his nose in a conspiratorial gesture. "Of course, what you really could use is an associate on the inside.

Wonder if there are any of your father's companions still running belowground and dealing on the dark side of the law."

Martin felt the blood rush from his face, leaving him momentarily cold. With his next inhale, all the heat flooded back, burning his skin in a flush of shame. How dare Mr. Collier suggest that Martin might deal with the kind of men his father had worked alongside—with the kind of men his father had been. As a fence, Martin Harrison Sr. had offered thieves and cutpurses a place to conceal their stolen goods, sometimes selling them himself and sometimes merely hiding them until the thieves sold them to other criminals.

Martin straightened himself and said with no hint of the friendliness with which Collier addressed him, "Apologies, sir, but I do not do business with criminals, no matter whom they used to know."

"Ah, naturally," Collier said, giving Martin a sage nod. "Nor do I, nor do I." His grin belied his assertion, and his continuous, pigeon-like bobbing of his head erased all credibility Martin held for the man. "But I will not deny that having an associate or two in the underworld is the best way to get important information. Sometimes the newspapers get lucky, but nothing beats an ear to the ground when it comes to passing word of illegal doings."

Was the man suggesting that the Manchester constabulary regularly made deals with criminals?

Collier continued speaking and, if not actually answering Martin's unspoken question, made himself clearer. "We've already heard some rumblings around town. People asking questions. Questions about paintings and storage and provenance."

"Provenance?" Martin recalled Rosanna using that term, but he was unsure what it meant.

Wiggins spoke up. "When serious buyers purchase paintings, they often look for authenticated pieces. Sometimes it's as simple as tacking a paper to the back of the frame that lists the painting's buyers and sellers through history. Other pieces are more difficult to tie to a legitimate seller."

Martin nodded once more to Wiggins. "I thank you for your assistance at Cheetham Hill. And as for uncovering any further information on our man—"

Collier interrupted. "I'll handle that part. If someone's doing shadowy business on our city streets, one of our men ought to have heard about it. Vladimir Blackbridge, you said?"

"Anton Greystone." Martin was unable to keep a note of frustration out of his voice. "Perhaps you might write it down."

Martin caught Wiggins's friendly wink as the older man retreated from the vestibule.

Collier scratched the name in a notebook and nodded again. "Greystone. Rings a bell. Seems as though someone warned us about him. I believe we have put a few men quietly on his trail already. One name I won't have to make note of is yours, Mr. Harrison. It's not every day that one of our most famous criminals returns to us voluntarily." He slapped Martin on the shoulder with a look of good humor upon his face.

No part of the joke pleased Martin, who shook his head. "I am not my father," he said. "And I am no criminal."

Collier laughed, as if Martin had told a joke. "And a good

thing, too, for we've proved we can catch Martin Harrison. You had best watch yourself."

Pressing his anger down inside himself, Martin said, "Perhaps as a function of growing up without my father, I have become accustomed to following a strict moral code, which allows me to excel at my job, as I am sure you excel at yours. I shall be off now. I appreciate your assistance."

Collier was undeterred by Martin's correction or his attempt to excuse himself. He placed his arm over Martin's shoulder and said, "How long since you've seen your old dad?"

If there was anything Martin was less inclined to discuss with Mr. Collier, he had no idea what it might be. "A long time." He stepped nearer to the door.

Collier nodded. "Right, right. He was sent to Australia, if I'm not mistaken?"

Martin nodded. "You are not mistaken, sir. I ought to be going."

Mr. Wiggins reentered the vestibule, a folded paper card in his hand. "Inspector," he said, handing the card to Martin. "The next train to Liverpool departs soon."

Martin bowed his thanks both for the information and the excuse to leave the constabulary.

"Good luck to you, young Martin Harrison," Collier said, and as Martin left, he could hear Collier laughing about the irony of a criminal spawning a Peeler. The jocularity of Mr. Collier, common in several of the constabulary offices Martin had worked in, landed with a particular edge. Never had the brotherly jokes and good-natured teasing brought with them such a stab of pain.

Martin had begun to hope for a place here in Manchester at the end of the exhibition's run, but if the cost was hearing mockery about his father, he was not sure he wanted to pay the price.

Glancing at the railway schedule in his hand, Martin saw that Wiggins's warning about the train's imminent departure was a slight understatement. If he were to intercept the locomotive, he would need to go at a run.

He pressed his hat upon his head and vaulted himself into the street.

CHAPTER 18

ROSANNA HEARD A CHURCH bell toll the hour and began to run. She knew she must look a sight, hauling her large, wrapped packages through the Manchester streets at a trot, but she did not care.

She muttered encouragement to herself. "You can do it, Rosie. Go. Hurry. You can make it." Rounding a corner, she bumped into a young man walking toward her. He apologized and offered his help.

"Thank you, no. I don't need anything," she said over her shoulder as she hurried away.

But that was not exactly true. She could certainly have used a few things. Time, for one. The ability to race through the city without gasping, for another. Not to mention the expertise, experience, or knowledge of how to reclaim stolen artwork.

With every thought, Rosanna's discouragement grew.

What was she thinking? How could she possibly repair this problem she had allowed to form?

This was a matter for the police.

For Inspector Martin Harrison.

Mr. Harrison who would almost certainly head straight to the constabulary, sending a Peeler to escort her from the locked office in the exhibition hall to a different locked room where she could remain under careful watch.

Oh, dear.

She hoped the man who discovered the empty office would not be berated for her disappearance.

A train whistle blew, snapping Rosanna's mind back to the matter at hand. She needed to find out if Anton was aboard the train to Liverpool. She ran on, her heart beating faster with each step.

Approaching the station, she saw people milling casually along the platform beside the rails. Her heart thudded as it always did in the presence of the gigantic locomotives. She did not fear riding inside the machines themselves once they were underway, but she remembered what her parents had told her about the railway's opening day, and the tragic accident that had befallen a man who tried to run across the tracks to see an acquaintance in another train.

Her unique talent for visualizing images did not serve her well when the stories they told her became particularly explicit.

It was not only her parents. Neighbors and acquaintances all seemed to have at least one story about someone who knew someone who had lost a leg or worse on the rails. She had listened to these stories of railway tragedies and disasters, and consequently, when she was required to board a train, she felt ill and weak.

She could not talk herself out of the feeling. It was not as though the danger was simply imagined. Signs hung about every rail station demanding the constant vigilance of rail riders.

"If you follow the rules, you have no need to fear," her mother had often said following yet another horrible, moralistic story of someone disregarding simple safety directions.

Follow the rules? How could she take the slightest comfort from that now? As an integral player in a major art robbery, she was flaunting practically every moral and ethical instruction she had ever learned. And she had every intention of lying, stealing, and defrauding before the afternoon was done.

Certainly, her plan was to lie to a liar, steal something that had already been stolen, and defraud a fraudulent man, but how many hairs could she split and still call herself an honest woman?

Rosanna shook off that thought and entered the railway office. At the ticket window, she asked for passage to Liverpool.

The young man behind the window traded her money for a paper ticket, instructed her to hold on to it, and looked past her shoulder.

"Next?" he said, no sign of a smile on his lips.

"Wait, please," Rosanna said.

He redirected his attention to her.

She glanced around the ticketing office. "How can I know if someone has bought a ticket for this train?"

He looked confused. "Many people have done so, miss. We transport more passengers between cities than—"

She cut him off. "A particular person, I mean. I am

supposed to be meeting a friend." She could hear the shake in her voice. Friend, indeed. "Do you have a list of travelers today?"

He looked at her through narrowed eyes. "I did not ask your name, miss. Nor did I ask anyone else's. It is not the LMR's job, nor is it our habit, to arrange rendezvous between passengers. Seems like you and your friend did not plan too carefully when you decided to make this trip." His tone had turned to exasperation. Annoyance. Blame. He would remember this irritating woman who interrupted his busy afternoon. Precisely what she did not want.

She must remain invisible.

Forcing herself to maintain her composure, she arranged her face into what she hoped was an unremarkable blandness. The face of someone easily forgotten. Commonplace. Ordinary.

She nodded, trying to smile. "Right, of course. Well, then, I shall search the cars. Wish me luck!" Never had an attempt a lightness felt so heavy to Rosanna.

Passengers began to board the train in earnest. Several hundred people, if Rosanna's guess could be trusted. She tucked her wrapped paintings close to her body, folded her arms around them, and tried to blend in with the crowd.

She noticed porters lifting steamer trunks and hat boxes, and she assumed those were for passengers whose destinations went past Liverpool—those bound for an ocean liner, perhaps. Could one of those trunks hold the paintings? Anything larger than a bandbox became suspicious in her eyes.

She watched the workers for a moment as they tossed small boxes and hoisted larger trunks by leather straps, swinging them from the platform up into the arms of other men waiting to receive them. As each case disappeared into the train, Rosanna realized that none of them could belong to Anton. He would not let the paintings out of his sight, not for the entire train ride. Not even for a minute.

If he was on the train, the paintings were with him.

Rosanna joined the queue of passengers and walked up the metal steps into the train. Immediately she felt the familiar rush of blood as fear pushed sparks into her arms and legs. She forced herself to walk through a car that felt far too full, then stepped out the door and onto the connecting bridgeway to the next car.

Even at a standstill, the tiny platform made of grated metal was the very image of danger. Through the floor, Rosanna could see the rails, the wooden beams, the rocks and dirt. Those very rails may have been the place the people in the stories met their gruesome ends.

She needed to step over the gap. Each car was coupled to the next by a beam no thicker than a man's leg. Someone pushed past her as she stood rooted to the connecting walkway. With nothing but the door to cling to, Rosanna flattened herself against the car's exterior and squeezed her eyes closed. Hot waves of panic rushed over her. She gasped for breath.

More passengers moved through the small doorway beside her, stepping across the bridgeway as though it were a path on any street. They seemed to think nothing of it, and each of them survived the three-step journey without incident. When a tiny, elderly couple nodded hello as they passed her, she forced herself to lift her feet. If they could do it, she could most certainly do it.

She gulped down her terror, closed her eyes, and followed the couple across the connection. At the door of the next car, she breathed again.

Many of the passengers moved straight through the car, but she was unsure why. It seemed perfect, with plenty of seats on either side of the aisle. She had just taken a seat near the center when the reason for the empty car became clear.

The ghastly smell.

Unwilling to spend more time in the railcar surrounded by the stench, she followed the stream of passengers to the back door, feeling another flush of terror at crossing the bridgeway. This time, however, she was already holding her breath. She closed her eyes and blindly passed over the grated floor with everyone else. The fear still gripped her, but the whole affair was certainly quicker.

At the entrance to the third car, she took a sip of air, grateful for the familiar, usual odors of crowds. This car was filling quickly, and Rosanna scanned the seats for a glimpse of a familiar black beard. There was no sign of Anton Greystone in this car either.

Had he managed to escape the city earlier? Or by some other way?

Might she have misjudged his intention? Perhaps he had stayed in Manchester after all.

Rosanna exited the car and stepped across the connecting platform, feeling a ripple run up the back of her neck. Someone was watching her.

Foolish, she thought. She was in a busy rail station. Of

course someone was watching. The people were all watching each other, taking in the surroundings. It was the very definition of being in a crowd.

But this felt different. More specific.

She kept her face forward and stepped into the car. Her eyes immediately went to a man a few paces away. She had seen him outside Mrs. Whitmore's boardinghouse, leaning against a wall. He must be an associate of Anton's.

He was trying to appear nonchalant, as though he did not see her, but she knew he had been staring at her only seconds before. Rosanna wanted to glare directly at him, to catch him in his game of pretending not to watch her. Instead, she forced her gaze to skim over the passengers as if she, like everyone else, only sought a seat.

There was no need to tip her hand.

The man, wearing a nondescript black coat and hat, sat at a window, book in one hand and quizzing glass in the other. Rosanna scoffed at the affectation. Perhaps he would do better to face the world head-on rather than look at the world through a tiny magnifier. He might see something he needed to learn.

Feeling that such a suggestion would also help her—surely *she* needed to face the world and learn from her own foolish mistakes—she glanced again across the seats. Before she had scanned half the car, she saw him.

Anton.

She was not convinced he had seen her. He had not seemed startled, but perhaps she *had* been noticed—just not by Anton himself. It was a crowded car. People were still jostling, pushing their way past other passengers and vying for seats and space for their bags.

Rosanna slid into a seat on the opposite side of the train, angling herself so she could keep a casual eye on Anton without turning around or craning her neck.

After a moment, another man in a nondescript coat and hat sat beside her. Her heart jumped, but she could not mistrust every person in a crowded train car. Simply because this man was dressed like the man she had noticed upon entering the car did not mean they were connected. She shifted slightly closer to the window.

He removed his hat. "Hello," he said, a stiffness to his voice suggesting he did not generally make conversation with strangers.

Rosanna gave a small but polite smile.

As he smiled in return, a gold tooth glinted behind his lip. A gold tooth much like Anton's. Rosanna suppressed a shudder.

The stranger offered to place her packages on a rack above their seats, but she shook her head. "I thank you, sir, but I'd rather keep them close."

His legs reached the seat facing them, blocking her from making a quick exit.

"Something precious, is it?" he asked, leaning closer.

"Only to me," she said. Oh, dear, she thought. Had she placed herself in danger? The thought almost made her laugh. She had escaped police custody only an hour earlier. Now she sat twelve seats away from Anton Greystone, who, at their last meeting, had both threatened and bruised her. She was already knee-deep in danger.

Adjusting the packages, she tightened her grip on them.

A sharp shriek of the whistle and an announcement from a uniformed railway worker told her that they would be moving soon.

Another man took the seat opposite Rosanna. He nodded, then pulled his hat down over his eyes. He stretched his legs in a diagonal line, effectively trapping her in her seat. With his arms crossed, he appeared to fall asleep instantly. Rosanna felt a crush of claustrophobia at being closed into her tiny corner.

Think about something else, she commanded herself. *Consider your plan.*

She intended to confront Anton after the Patricroft stop, just between Cromwell Road and the Bridgewater canal. She assumed many of the travelers would have disembarked by that point, leaving fewer passengers to witness any scene she might cause. Waiting until they were at the edge of the city would prevent Anton an easy escape from the train. Then she would demand that he return the Michelangelo, the Cole, and the Gainsborough to the exhibition hall.

And what, she thought, would be his response?

She closed her eyes and sighed. At the very best, he would scoff.

At worst . . .

Well, she dared not think of the worst.

He would not hurt her, though. She was sure of that.

She was *almost* sure of that.

His last visit to her rooms had caused her to rethink much of what she had known about Anton Greystone.

How foolish of her to think that Anton would respond to

a polite request to return three paintings with anything other than laughter.

And yet, here she sat, closed into a window seat in a train car filled with people. Somewhere on this train were the original paintings, but there was no way she could recover them.

Perhaps she could ask another passenger to request the paintings. She could send one of these men beside her to demand Anton give over the three paintings, to menace him if needed.

But what if he had more than three? What if there were boxes and boxes of stolen paintings?

A lump grew in her throat. Mind whirring, Rosanna tried to maintain her composure. It would certainly not be helpful if she fell into a swoon or began to sob.

She was not trained to enforce the law; she was no Peeler. She had no practical experience catching criminals. Nor was she a sneaky, clever thief. None of her skills had prepared her for this, and she had far overestimated her own cleverness. Now, in the face of certain danger, she had nothing but a couple of pretty paintings clutched in her arms.

Think, she told herself. *Come up with an idea.*

But she knew it was no good. Creating was not her talent. She was a reproductionist. She imitated. She copied. She did not invent. Neither her ideas nor her productions were original.

Her original ideas had led only to ridicule and mockery. Her attempts to paint what was in her heart made people uncomfortable. And comfort was, as it turned out, what people most desired, both in their art and in their lives.

Comfort in what they understood. In what they saw. In what they knew. In all that they experienced.

Never had the truth been so clear to Rosanna as it was now. When she had broken out of the locked office, she was eager to rush to recover the lost paintings, excited even. But now, she wished beyond anything to be home in her rooms, imitating paintings that someone else decided were comfortable.

Excitement was completely overrated.

Rosanna felt herself growing warm. These men were so close, and the train car was so full. And there, much too near to hide from, sat Anton, holding his own silly quizzing glass and turning the pages of a penny dreadful, looking for all the world like a former soldier settling back into life at home.

But Anton Greystone was not as he appeared, just like the paintings he passed off as originals. He was an imitation himself, a slicked-up presentation of a man he would never be. His soldier's beard might fool someone into believing he had served in the Crimean, but the image of a former soldier did not tell a particle of his truth. Just as Rosanna's reproductions lacked the work of formulation, Anton lacked the depth of character and experience of the man he would like people to see.

Rosanna's paintings did not require her to prepare. She did not need to work to compose the image, to study the fall of light, to distribute visual weight throughout the canvas. She simply saw what was already accomplished and copied it.

Copied. The word she always resented. But what was her work, really? She was following in another artist's brilliance, imitating brushstrokes and color. The genius of the work was not in its production, but in its creation.

And Rosanna Hawkins created nothing.

Nothing but a great deal of trouble at the moment.

The heat became oppressive. She wished to let down the glass in the window beside her, but there was no latch, no handle by which to remove the pane.

Not daring to stand, she squirmed in her seat. She could not let Anton see her before she was ready to face him, and at this moment, she was very, very unready to face him.

Her wiggling drew the attention of the man beside her.

"All right, miss? D'you need something?" he asked, a slight sneer on his face offering another glimpse of the gold tooth.

Martin had asked her that question so often, checking to see if she was well, and she had always felt protected by his solicitation, if amused by his persistence. Strange how a tone of voice could carry intent. Rosanna's skin crawled with revulsion at the inquiry now.

"Perhaps just a bit of air," she said, pressing herself against the window to keep herself from touching him. Her skirts covered the feet of both men and took up far more than her fair share of the compartment space.

"Perhaps a short walk would do you good," he said, reaching out a hand to grip her upper arm.

She pulled away, shaking her head. "No, thank you. I simply need more breathing room."

He tightened his grasp on her arm. Standing up, he pulled her to her feet. "I believe," he said, practically snarling the words into her ear, "you will take a walk with me."

Rosanna stumbled over the legs of the sleeping man, who suddenly was not sleeping at all.

"That's right," he said, stepping behind her, pinning her between the two of them. As he leaned forward to hiss into her ear, she felt his hot breath. "There's someone on this train what wants to see you."

Rosanna pulled in a gasp of air, hoping she could manage a scream loud enough to inspire the nearby passengers to help her.

As though he could read her thoughts, the man behind her touched her back with something sharp and said, "Let's not make any fuss, shall we? Wouldn't want to slip. Someone could get hurt."

Rosanna understood his implication immediately. She swallowed her scream and allowed the men to guide her along the aisle of the car, stopping at the row where Anton Greystone sat. He replaced the quizzing glass in his pocket and the penny dreadful upon his lap, then smiled up at her.

"Hello, Bunny. What a delight to find you here."

CHAPTER 19

As Martin made his way to the train station, he fumed. Collier had insulted him in almost every way. As though being the son of a criminal made him somehow susceptible to illegal behavior. The very idea.

Martin shuddered at the thought that, perhaps, Collier would send a tail to watch him.

Were Collier's witticisms about the return of Martin's father somehow meant as warnings?

Pushing his way through the streets, he thought how utterly foolish it would be for a man in his position to try a life of crime. Nonsense.

Yet, the further the idea sank in, Martin could see how it might hold some merit. Not for him, of course. He abhorred duplicity in any form, particularly the use of falsehoods to hurt people. But if he were a different kind of man, perhaps his prisoner father would be the perfect cover.

A man like Martin, with the appearance of an upright officer of the law, could likely secure the trust of all manner of people, both within the underground communities of criminals and among the upright citizens. With that trust, he could, should the opportunity present itself, insert himself into confidence schemes ranging from the simple swindle to something of incredible magnitude. Like lifting priceless paintings from a gallery, for instance.

Martin shook his head.

What in the world had him thinking this way?

His moral compass pointed true north, always.

But the possibility existed. When there was an easy way to make money, there would always be someone who would step into that simple path. And some were naturally suited, by temperament or situation, to take advantage of others.

He wondered what advantages of this kind Miss Hawkins may have had. Did her parents have connections to an unsavory element? Had she joined up with Greystone because of some flaw of her parents?

He hoped there was some excuse to explain her behavior, but even excuses of family could not justify her dishonorable actions, more's the pity.

Martin knew that whatever *he* gained of money, respect, or station, he would have to earn. Particularly in this city, where his name would always carry the shadow of his father's infamy.

The train's whistle pierced the air, and Martin broke into a jog. He moved toward the center of the street, eager to hurry past the meandering crowd.

It always struck him as strange how people congregated in slow-moving groups precisely where others needed clear spaces to hurry.

At a particularly congested street corner, a middle-aged

woman in a vibrant blue plaid ensemble broke from the crowd and waved toward him.

"Inspector," she called, motioning him to come to where she stood with a dozen others.

Martin glanced toward the railway station and then back to the people huddled in a group. He must not miss the train, but he recognized her concern.

He moved toward the woman as she came to him.

"Oh, Inspector, how quickly you've responded," she said, pressing her hand to his uniform jacket's arm.

Martin shook his head, breathing hard from his hurry. "I did not, that is, I was not . . . I beg pardon, ma'am," he said, unable to form a complete sentence.

The woman, ignoring his confusion, took him by the arm and bustled him over to the knot of people on the corner. Her voluminous skirts swished around his legs, and he had to take care not to stumble over them.

"Here he is," she told Martin, assuming once again that he had any understanding of what she needed.

A man, probably approaching sixty years, sat upon the ground, one hand rubbing his sparse, white hair, the other clutching his shirtfront.

"Knocked him right down, it did," the woman said. "Poor dear."

"Outrageous, the way these young people operate their carriages," the man muttered. "In my day—"

At the sound of yet another whistle from the train, Martin seized upon the man's lamentation to make his escape.

"Sir, if you are relatively unhurt, I shall try to discover the perpetrator. Allow these fine people to care for you until another officer arrives, which should be at any moment. Meanwhile, I will . . ." Martin, poised to chase, as far as these people knew, after the offending carriage driver, nodded at the crowd and dashed away.

At a run, he darted through the streets toward the station, feeling a tiny prick of compunction for allowing those people to believe he was apprehending a careless driver. Had there been enough time, he would have explained that a bigger fish was, at that very moment, likely settled into a seat on the train.

The train that was now pulling away from the station.

Martin increased his speed, brushing past people who lingered at the platform and waved at passengers who were pressed against rapidly disappearing windows.

Allowing himself a mild whispered curse, Martin kept running past the station, its building and platform crowded with people. He could not outrun the train once it gained its full speed, but that would still take several minutes. And he could run for several more minutes.

A Peeler on the train platform stepped into his path and shouted for him to slow down, but Martin only saluted, hoping the officer would take note of his uniform.

He jumped down from the platform and ran along the rails, feet pounding the rocks and cinders along the side.

Time seemed to stretch and pull back all at once. Each hammering step thudded in time with Martin's heart, but the blow of the whistle seemed to extend on for minutes, hours, days in his head. Lungs and legs burning, he pushed himself to move faster and faster.

How had he never noticed how loud train yards were?

Not only the piercing whistles and the clanging bells but also the overwhelming noise of thousands of pounds of metal pressing on metal, driven by the power of something as ephemeral as steam.

Tucking his head to focus on the ground beneath his feet, Martin realized he was muttering to himself in time with his footsteps, encouraging his own speed. Moments that felt like instants and years sped and dragged him forward as he gained on the train.

At any moment the train's speed would increase faster than he could possibly match.

It was now. Now or never, he thought, but then retracted the last words. Never was not an option. *Now.*

A burst of speed brought him to the side of the last car. Holding his breath, he caught the handle at the doorway and lifted his feet from the ground. Pulling himself tight against the side of the train with both arms, he kicked at the door, which swung open. Martin stumbled inside and practically fell into the lap of an elderly woman sitting on the aisle side of the last row.

She let out a squeak of surprise, and he saw her take in his uniform as she pressed him away from her.

"Pardon, ma'am," he gasped. He touched his forehead and moved down the aisle, gathering his breath and searching the faces of each passenger as they looked up at him.

He had done it. He had chased down a moving railroad car and leaped onto it.

Unsure whether it was every boy's dream come true, he knew it was certainly one of his. He took a moment to bask in the thrilling rush that sailed through his body. He wished there was someone he could tell. Someone to share the dangerous delight of the moment.

If only Rosanna Hawkins had been here to see it.

Shaking his head, Martin tried to dislodge the ever-present thought of Miss Hawkins. How could that possibly help him now?

Martin's steps slowed in time with his heartbeat, but then his breath caught.

He had no idea what his quarry looked like. Any one of the men on this train—or none of them—could be Anton Greystone.

At the connecting door to the next car, Martin stepped across the gangway. One of the engineering staff stood, arms folded, with his back to the adjoining door.

Martin's breath still ragged, he tapped the man on the shoulder. "Sir, a word?" he said, and motioned to the door.

"You want to have a chat out there?"

"Unless there is another place where we could discuss a pressing and private security matter," Martin said, struggling to keep his voice steady as he forced his breath into a more uniform rhythm.

The man nodded and followed Martin out to the gangway.

Martin wasted no more time. "I am Inspector Martin Harrison."

"Ned Pilgrim, sir," the man said.

"Ned, there may be a dangerous criminal on board this train."

Pilgrim stood up straighter, a look of surprise covering his face. "Sir?"

"As well as stolen property," Martin finished. He realized that was the extent of what he felt sure about. And that *sure* was shaky at best.

"Very well, sir," Ned Pilgrim said. "Who is the man?"

"His name is Anton Greystone," Martin said, the voice of Collier invoking Mr. Dickens's name loud in his memory. "Or at least that is the name by which he chooses to be known."

Ned nodded and pulled a stub of pencil and a small notebook from his breast pocket. Martin saw him scribble the name.

"What does he look like, sir?"

Martin felt a fool. "Ahem." He cleared his throat. "He may be in disguise."

It was possible, Martin told himself. Even so, he felt a twinge of shame at the disingenuous answer.

"And his age?" Ned Pilgrim asked, pencil poised.

"It could be a very convincing disguise."

Ned slowly lowered his pencil.

Martin took a deep breath and said, "May I have your permission to walk through each car and make an assessment of the passengers?"

Ned pointed to Martin's uniform. "I don't think you need my permission, sir. You certainly outrank me, so as far as I'm concerned, you may do as you please."

"Thank you." Martin nodded at the man and stepped back into the second car.

As soon as he began looking at each passenger, the excuse he'd given Ned Pilgrim began to grow in his mind. All he knew about Greystone had come from Miss Hawkins, and she had not offered much detail. Martin held the impression that Greystone and Miss Hawkins were closely connected, and therefore he had assumed that Anton Greystone would be a young man, like himself; fit and strong, like himself; possessed of a reasonable attractiveness, like himself.

Martin passed through the train car looking for . . . himself.

What utter nonsense.

At each train car Martin entered, he spoke quietly to the staff member posted at the door. Each nodded him through. With a growing sense of failure, Martin moved down each car's aisle. None of the passengers appeared to be master thieves. None appeared particularly nervous or anxious.

Martin stepped through the last door, and his eyes instantly fastened upon a woman being escorted down the train car's aisle by two men.

Even from behind, he was certain who she was.

That form was indelibly etched in his mind. He knew that dress. He knew that step. And he knew, without a shadow of doubt, that hair, piled into a mass of curls and stuck through with pencils and paintbrushes.

Somehow, against every particle of reason and possibility, Rosanna Hawkins was walking in front of him. Rosanna, whom he had locked in an office at the Art Treasures Exhibition mere hours ago. Rosanna, who had led him to search for Anton Greystone.

Rosanna, who was now slipping into a seat beside a strikingly handsome man with a black beard. Rosanna, who was leaning her face forward to give that man a kiss.

CHAPTER 20

ROSANNA TILTED HER CHIN up and gave Anton a smile she hoped he would see as sincere.

It was all she could do not to wipe that kiss off her mouth.

He looked at her, a corner of his mouth quirked in a smile beneath his mustache, giving no indication of whether or not he trusted her.

After a moment, he nodded at the man who still held Rosanna's shoulder. The man backed away, and Rosanna felt her breathing ease a fraction, though her heart still pounded. She placed her two wrapped packages on the floor by her feet.

"You weren't going to go away without me, were you?" she said, pouting her lips and ducking down her chin so she could look up at him through her eyelashes. If he wanted a bunny, she would give him a bunny. She drew a hand along the V of his vest.

Right where his heart would be, she thought. *If he had one.*

As if in response to her thought, he straightened, moving fractionally away from her.

She stayed as steady as the moving train allowed her to, her hand spread across his vest, gazing up at him, unwilling to be the first to look away. She needed him to believe her sincerity.

She worried she might strain something, keeping her neck tilted like this.

Anton glanced at the men surrounding them, then returned his gaze to Rosanna. "I was under the impression that you were planning on taking the business of your work into your own hands. After our last meeting, I did not think you were interested in working together anymore."

Sighing, she shook her head. "Upon careful reconsideration, I recognize that I have my talents—and you have yours. Either of us without the other is simply less. Less likely to be successful, less persuasive. You know that I need you," she said with a simper, the words tasting like vinegar on her tongue.

He did not answer, which was just as well. She needed to add a few more layers.

"There is a reason we are such a perfect team. A partnership. Your strength making up for my weaknesses. Give and take. Your gifts and mine," she said, offering another uncomfortable—but hopefully convincing—tilt of her head and an utterly contrived fluttering of her eyelashes. "Do not think about the silly things I said before."

She leaned closer and tucked her head onto his shoulder, relieving herself of the burden of eye contact. "Please leave my mistakes in the past," she said, pulling his arm around her waist. "I cannot bear to think that you remember the foolish things I did. We ought to think only of the future."

With one arm around her, he was exactly half as likely to surprise her with his movements. There was no comfort in his embrace, no warmth, but there was small safety in knowing where at least one of his hands was.

From this new vantage point, she could see Inspector Harrison sitting at the far end of the car. A wave of both surprise and relief washed over her. He was here. Exactly as she had hoped. He had removed his hat and coat, and without his uniform, he did not look like a policeman. But he did not move toward her. What was he waiting for? She rearranged herself upon the seat and, fastening her gaze on Anton's beard, she lay a finger along the side of her nose.

Please, she thought. *Let Martin see it. Let him remember the sign.*

"Where are we heading?" Rosanna asked, hoping Anton could not hear the tremble in her voice.

"Liverpool." His reply was curt, but he did not move away.

"And from there?" she asked, reaching up and stroking his beard, that false symbol of soldierly bravery.

The single huff of breath that escaped Anton might have been a chuckle had it been repeated. As it was, she did not think him amused.

Patience, she told herself.

As the train swayed, she slipped one arm behind Anton's back.

She let her words fall slowly, matching the rhythmic rocking of the train car. "I should like to see Europe through your eyes," she whispered into his ear. "Paris and Florence, Berlin and Amsterdam."

At that last, she felt his back stiffen. Amsterdam. Right. Very well.

"Wherever the next adventure takes you, I want to be there with you."

He hummed a note that might have been an assent and turned his head to place a kiss atop her head. With his slight shift, she felt the handle of the pocket-sized pistol in his vest. The train rocked again, side to side.

"We both know that many people can paint pretty pictures like I can," she said, surprising herself with the ease of her simpering tone. "But is there anyone else who knows you the way I do?"

She did not truly want him to answer that so she continued, reminding herself to keep using a quiet, breathy voice.

"A few sales will set you up for quite some time, I am sure," she said. "But if you had a constant supply of materials—my reproductions—nothing could stop you from becoming the Continent's most prolific dealer." Her hand crept into the pocket, resting on the grip of the gun. "No one can match your talents for selling art. No one."

At the next serious sway of the train car, she lifted the pistol and shoved it into the corner of his seat. Her heart thumped in her ears, pounding in time with the sounds of the wheels on the track.

"As in any business, you ought to expect compensation." She shifted toward the aisle so he could see her face. "And not every compensation is monetary." She smiled at him and stood, one hand grasping his.

She glanced behind Anton at his henchmen who had practically dragged her up the aisle. She hoped there was not another of his men behind her, for she knew she must stop stalling. Stop talking. She simply could not bring herself to say more. Her mouth tasted bitter with the repulsive words she had already uttered.

Using her other hand hidden behind her back, she gestured to the man at the other end of the car.

If Inspector Martin Harrison was not watching, so help her, she might scream.

There was only so long she could remain swaying on her feet, Anton's thugs standing down but at the ready.

Anton held her eyes, and his mouth twisted in a mocking grin. "What makes you think it must be you?"

She could not discern if he meant to be cruel, or if this was his idea of flirtation.

She turned fully toward him, a hand on either shoulder, and leaned in until their faces nearly touched. She fluttered her eyelashes. "Mr. Greystone," she said, smiling, "you have seen me at work." She pressed her lips ever so lightly to his and then backed an inch away. "But you have not"—she kissed his mouth again—"seen all"—her hands slid down his arms—"I can do." One hand landed on the leather seat at his back.

She kissed him once more, her hand closing around his pistol and removing it from the corner of the seat. She kept her eyes locked on his as she tucked her arm behind her back.

She straightened up. Her heart was pounding, and if Anton's expression was any indication, his pulse was racing also. Jaw slackened, eyes dewy, he looked at her in wonder. But was it the wonder of infatuation? Or did he suspect her of nefarious dealings?

She waggled the pistol behind her back, and before she could think of anything else to say to Anton, she felt it lifted from her hand as a shoulder brushed past her. She brought her now-empty hands to Anton's shoulders and smiled at him, a smile that was far more sincere now that Anton was disarmed.

She watched from the corner of her eye as Martin Harrison stepped past the motley collection of Anton's men and secured the gun into his own waistcoat. He looked for an empty seat, but when he couldn't find one, he turned to retrace his steps down the aisle.

"I can scarcely sit still for excitement," she said, shuffling her feet beneath her skirts before sliding back into the seat next to Anton. "Now, I must confess, I have not come on this adventure completely prepared, especially if we are boarding a ship for the Continent. However, I have brought something that I think you will like." She forced herself to grin.

One of his eyebrows raised in question.

She reached to the floor and pulled her packages into her lap. "And what do you suppose these might be?" she asked in a teasing voice. All her will was focused on maintaining a giddy grin and a light tone.

When Anton did not answer, she said, "Perhaps I was mistaken. Perhaps these hold no interest for you at all." She carefully averted her gaze. A forced pout. Another flutter of her eyelashes.

See, Mother? Your money was well spent. The governess taught me more than painting and French.

She moved to place the packages back onto the floor, but Anton took her wrists in his hands. Though far more gently than the last time he had laid hands on her, he still gripped her tightly enough that she was unable to move. She did not fight.

"What have you brought me?"

His tone was impossible to read. Was he excited? Amused? Annoyed?

"Clear some room, and I'll show you." She fought to keep her voice steady.

Anton nodded to the people on the surrounding benches, including the facing seats, and four men in total moved from their places.

Reaching for the packages, Anton seemed surprised when she flinched and moved them away from him. His eyes, squinting at her, held a shadow of his violent anger.

She forced a smile. "Gently," she murmured.

Placing one of the packages across her knees and the other atop it, she carefully and slowly unwrapped the one on top. At the sight of her reproduced Michelangelo, Anton's face lit up. What she had once interpreted as joy she now recognized as greed, an eagerness to seize what her work would bring him.

She hoped this one would bring him something he could not anticipate, had not ever dreamed of.

Smiling, hoping she knew what she was doing, she unwrapped the second. She laid them side by side on the facing seat.

"I did these two from memory, hoping to have something to hold on to after the exhibition ended," she lied. "But I realized they would be far better appreciated and more valued by someone else."

She watched his face closely, hoping he believed her. "If they could be studied by guests of an important family, or even hung in a public place where others would see them, so many more people could enjoy being in the presence of great work. Or a mimicry of great work," she added with what she hoped was a convincing show of modesty.

He leaned forward and touched the edge of the boards with a proprietary motion. "What exactly did you have in mind?" he asked, his voice low. Was his tone dangerous, or reverent?

"Oh, I cannot judge the best path forward. You know far better than I how to get my little copies into the hands of people who would value them." The words slipped out of her mouth with no evidence of the price it cost her to say them. She fisted her hands and tucked them under the voluminous folds of her skirts.

Nodding, he leaned closer and gazed at the paintings. The train rolled into another station, squealing to a stop. Rosanna took advantage to stand up again. It was far too difficult, too frightening to remain seated next to Anton for such a long stretch.

"I should like to compare them to the others I did. The ones I painted for you," she said, hoping that the memory of his exit from her rooms was not as present in his mind as it was in hers. "I am confident they are very alike."

Very alike, indeed. They were perfect.

He glanced at the metal luggage rack above his head, and she knew she need not pretend she did not understand him. "Oh, good." She beamed. "They're here with you? I'm so very glad." She reached for the large cloth sack, much like a soldier's carryall, that lay on the framework above them.

Heart stuttering, hands shaking, she waited for the inevitable moment Anton would stand and pull the bag from her hands, but he let her unfasten it, pull two swathed packages from it, and unwrap them.

She lay the two other *Madonna*s she had carried onto the train next to the others on the now-crowded double seat. Her heart lurched as she lifted what she knew was the original in her bare hands. She ought not to be touching this. No one ought to touch it without gloves. It ought not be here, in the open, among rough people like Anton's henchmen.

But better that it received a bit of unprotected contact than for it to disappear forever into the seedy European criminal underworld.

Gazing upon each detail, she lifted one painting, lay it down, lifted the next. She held her breath as she put her face close to Michelangelo's original, as if the very air from her lungs might harm it. For all she knew, it might.

Then she raised two of the boards, one in each hand, and leaned them against the seat back. As she did so, she shifted the others upon the seat, effectively shuffling the paintings. She pretended to study the upright copies. Shaking her head, she lifted one, placed another one in its spot, and stared deeply at it.

This had better work, she thought. People in the nearby seats had begun to lean in, watching her at first with that false, studied inattention one gives fellow passengers on trains, but soon with more interest.

If only she had been given lessons in street games and

confidence schemes. What was she doing now, after all, but a large-scale, priceless version of thimblerig, or the shell game? But instead of hiding a tiny ball in a thimble, she was attempting to con a con man.

Was there any chance Anton could tell the Michelangelo from her reproductions? Did he have any idea what she was doing? Her heartbeat throbbed in her throat, making it difficult to breathe.

Several passengers had gathered around the seats, crowding the aisle. Rosanna pretended not to notice the way Anton's men leaned forward, blocking bystanders out. She pretended to stay completely focused on the paintings and not see the way Anton waved his men off, accepting and even welcoming the audience.

With a few more shuffles of the paintings, she had the original Michelangelo on the outside of the seat and a crowd of onlookers leaning in.

The crowd included one specific man who had removed his coat and hat. He stood near Rosanna's seat, watching with his arms folded across his chest. As the train lurched forward, she felt his knee knock softly against her own, and a wave of relief washed over her. Martin was there to protect her. To protect the painting, of course, but also for her. She did not know if the inspector still wanted her jailed, but at least she was certain he did not want her dead. Small comfort, but comfort nonetheless to have him nearby.

A woman who had stood to watch Rosanna shuffle the paintings leaned in. "Were those for sale at the exhibition?" she asked. "I never noticed. I should have liked to purchase one."

A murmur of assent rippled through the small crowd. It seemed several of the gathered onlookers had visited the galleries, and this comment opened a dialogue among them.

"Right. I saw that one," a man said, pointing at the paintings. "By that fellow Ralph? Rafe? Whasisname?"

"I believe you are referring to Raphael," said a woman with a touch of asperity.

"But this one isn't by him," another man said. "This one is that Italian Donatello."

"No, the other man. Da Vinci."

Anton addressed the crowd. "These are extremely valuable reproductions, on their way to France for sale to the most exclusive salons." He nodded, punctuating his own words. "Many of the newly reinstated Parisian aristocrats are waiting for their own versions." He let this little gem penetrate the crowd for a moment before stroking his beard and looking around the assembly.

"But why," he asked, his rich voice working its usual captivating magic, "ought the French carry home all the prizes?" He was luring in an audience, but for what, Rosanna was unsure.

He slowed his words, adding a breath of tension to each phrase. "The French may originate many of the world's beauties, but they need not own them all."

The passengers, many of whom wore fashions that had originated in Paris, leaned in.

"And why ought the richest have exclusive access to all the best gifts?" Anton continued.

Rosanna noticed the collective nod ripple through the crowd, the jealous contempt of new money for old, which had been a hallmark of the area in which she and her sisters had grown up. These people had enough money to travel to see the Art Treasures Exhibition, but they were not wealthy enough to afford private conveyance. They might be bedecked in furs and layers of fabrics, but it was all a season or two behind the fashion.

"Perhaps I can allow myself to part with just one of these priceless images," Anton drawled, his voice taking on a lower tone and an even slower cadence as he swept his hand across the train seat filled with paintings. "For you, my friends, I believe I can allow one of them to grace the walls of an English home."

Murmurs of interest became voluble conversations, questions of cost, and verbal jostling for Anton's attention.

As each interested observer pressed in closer, Rosanna noticed that Inspector Harrison remained stationed directly behind her, his leg against her flowing skirts. Even if he was only here to rearrest her and throw her into the nearest lockaway, she felt safer knowing he was close. He might be angry, even furious, but he would not threaten or harm her. He would not strike her.

The train slowed for a stop at the Chat Moss embankment. Rosanna loved this stretch of bogland, near to towns but still ancient and primeval. Miles of lowlands, punctuated here and there by lone trees. The very sky felt larger here.

"Those of you who are not interested in making a valid offer may be best served to back away," Anton said, managing to dismiss the cash poor with his oily smile, allowing them to feel admired even as they were rejected.

Several travelers moved closer to the paintings. Rosanna

felt the heat from the press of bodies, but over all other concerns, she feared more people handling the antique masterpiece.

"If our price is right, you must be willing to sell more than one," a man said, nodding as though his demand was perfectly reasonable.

Anton gave a condescending chuckle, a sound that raised the short hairs on the back of Rosanna's neck. She had been on the receiving end of such laughs. They rarely signified humor.

"How shall you decide who will be allowed to purchase?" asked a woman.

Anton pushed past Rosanna's legs into the aisle and made himself the center of the circle of people. "I am a man of business," he said without apology. Spreading his hands in a magnanimous gesture, he added, "The prize, as it always does, goes to the highest offer."

As the train restarted its journey away from the Chat Moss platform, the small crowd of hopefuls began calling out amounts, rapidly and noisily outbidding each other. Anton's men took up positions around the bystanders, reinforcing the circle and leaving Rosanna alone with the paintings, unguarded.

Reaching for Anton's overcoat on the seat beside her, she surreptitiously slid it over the original Michelangelo, then stood and quickly turned away from the jostling crowd, handing the package over her seat back to Martin.

Pushing the coat and its treasure into his arms, she leaned up and pressed a kiss onto his lips.

"Go," she said.

Martin looked stunned.

She smiled at him. "Go," she repeated, this time with a small shove toward the door at the rear of the train. "Keep it safe."

The train picked up speed as Inspector Harrison opened the door, stepped off the gangway, and disappeared.

$\mathcal{C}$HAPTER 21

MARTIN JUMPED FROM the train's rear car and landed on the station platform with a jolt and a bit of a laugh. He had always wanted to do that. This day was filled with all manner of things he thought as a child that he would someday do as an officer.

Stopping to take stock, he shook out his shoulders and scanned the platform. Empty.

He had just put complete trust in a person who had escaped from imprisonment. Whether or not Rosanna Hawkins was now behaving within the bounds of decency he could not tell.

Was it possible she had handed him a counterfeit painting and shoved him from the train?

Certainly, it was possible.

Did that small kiss make the risk worthwhile?

Again, possible.

Oh, dear.

Martin smiled and shook his head. He pulled Greystone's coat away from the corner of board beneath. There was no way Martin could tell if what he held was an original, price-less artwork. Something in Rosanna's face made him believe she was helping him. Or at least she was helping to protect the Michelangelo.

Martin looked at the facts: He was holding a paint-ing that Rosanna had given to him. She had wrapped it in Greystone's overcoat. Moments, even seconds before, she had been snuggled into Greystone herself.

The facts did not bode well for Martin. But there had been truth in her eyes and on her lips as she pressed the parcel into Martin's hands. And the truth, though it contradicted the facts, spoke to her honesty. Her goodness. Rewrapping the painting in his arms, he moved from the tracks and looked around.

Chat Moss had changed little since he was a boy. The enormous peat bog held a few stumpy trees but little else. As he moved down the platform, he doubted many people utilized this stop.

As the train disappeared into the distance beneath a cloud of steam, he entered the station house. The room was deserted but for a young woman seated at a small desk.

"Pardon," Martin said.

She looked up.

"I need to send a message. This is a police emergency."

She glanced over him, and he remembered he had left his uniform coat and hat on the train.

Trying to sound official, he stood straighter. "I under-stand you can telegraph messages to other stations."

She tilted her head. "Sir, I am happy to send a message for you. You write it, and I'll add up the cost."

"The cost." His money was in his uniform coat, traveling west toward Liverpool.

Realizing he was holding Greystone's coat, he felt around it to see if there was a wallet in one of the pockets. Lumps and bulges within the fabric told Martin the coat had many more pockets than he would have expected. Glancing at the woman again, Martin unwrapped the coat from around the painting, settling the board gently on the floor and leaning it against the woman's desk. He held the coat up and ran his hands along the outside, finding the traditional two main pockets, which he emptied onto the small desk.

A train ticket, several coins, a pair of keys on a ring, a stub of pencil, two small notebooks, and a box of cigarette papers and tobacco. Feeling along the inside lining, he discovered three additional pockets, each padded with folded banknotes.

The woman's eyes widened at the mounting pile of money.

"I can send your message, sir," she said, her voice much more friendly now that she knew he could pay.

"Thank you. This message needs to be sent with utmost urgency up the line to every station all the way to Liverpool."

She nodded, pencil in hand.

"Police business. Thief onboard L&MR. Suspected of stealing priceless artworks from Manchester Exhibition. Spotted in last westbound car at Chat Moss station. Nearly six feet tall. Black beard and whiskers. Relieved of a pistol, but possibly still armed. Accompanied by several accomplices. Take care with the female accomplice, who already eluded Art Treasures Exhibition security."

The young woman wrote as quickly as he spoke, and now she looked up from the paper. "I can shorten this for you, save you a few pence."

He indicated the pile of money on the desk. "No need. Speed is worth the cost," he said, smiling. He knelt to wrap the painting again.

When she had finished keying in his message, Martin asked her, "Where is the nearest constabulary?"

"We've an officer in Astley, sir," she said, pointing vaguely eastward.

He nodded. "I shall need a message sent there, as well."

"Of course. Same message?"

Martin adjusted the words to best fit the audience. She took down his message without comment. He thanked her and requested yet another telegram sent.

"Manchester constabulary. To Wiggins."

She jotted down the name, then nodded her readiness.

"Recovered one stolen painting from the exhibition," he dictated. "Send officers to shore up security. Special guest need not be informed. Will catch next train back to Man."

The woman's eyes widened at each word, but she kept any opinion to herself. Martin wondered what story she was telling herself to make sense of these events. Could it come close to matching the truth?

Finished again, she asked Martin if he needed anything else.

"A ticket on the first return train to Manchester, please," he said.

He paid for his messages and his passage from Greystone's

money, then tallied up what he had spent, scrupulously keeping track so he could report it.

"One more thing," Martin said to the woman. "Is there a shop nearby in which I could find a safer way to transport my parcel?"

The woman shook her head. "Astley has a shop, but you'll not make it there and back before your train. Perhaps I could interest you in something from the leave-behind?"

He looked at her without responding for a moment. "I do not know what that means."

"It's what I call the things that get dropped or left or forgotten. Some things here have never been moved, not in years." She glanced around, as if someone might be watching, and added, "If it were not a matter of police business, I'd dare not offer, you understand."

She came around from her seat and led him to a door in the back wall. A tiny room, illuminated by filmy light through a dirty window, held a few crates, boxes, and piles of bags and coats.

He pointed to a corner. "Shoes?"

She nodded. "You might be surprised, sir."

He let out a small chuckle. "I am already surprised." He looked around. "Do people come back for these things?"

She shook her head. "Rarely, but I hold on to everything. Well," she added, looking a shade guilty, "I do chuck away food that might spoil."

He nodded and kept a serious expression, assuming she'd only confessed to him because he was an inspector. Though only a few minutes earlier, she had doubted him. He did not mind her skepticism. Too many people were fooled by unscrupulous pretenders. He would much rather deal with someone who challenged the statement "I am an officer of the law" than someone who trusted too easily.

"If I find a suitable case, might I borrow it?" he asked. "I would return it as soon as I am finished with it."

"Of course, of course," she said, pointing to a pile of canvas sacks. "There might be something there you can use."

Martin climbed over a few trunks and pulled the pile down piece by piece until he located a large canvas sack with handles. Pulling it over to the doorway, he opened it. Inside were books and bundles of papers.

"Any idea about these?" he asked.

The woman shrugged as she looked over the contents. "I had never thought to go through them, but perhaps if they're out of the bag, I could look into them a bit, maybe discover where they came from or who they belonged to."

Unloading the papers with care, Martin asked if there was a blanket or bedsheet in the room.

The woman knew exactly where to find what Martin was looking for, which did not surprise him. What else was there to do in this tiny station house, after all? She probably had a mental catalog of every left-behind item in her building.

She offered him two small quilts and a folded sheet of linen.

Wrapping the painting first in the blankets and then in the sheet, he slipped it into the bag. It was far easier to carry now, and he was grateful to have his hands free, as well as protection for the painting, whether it was the original or a copy. Either way, it was grandly done.

He took a seat in the small station house and allowed himself the first deep breath in a very long time.

Martin thought of Rosanna Hawkins, sitting before an easel with paintbrushes in her hands, behind her ears, tucked into her sleeves, dabbing pigment into canvas and onto boards to mimic the great paintings of other artists.

He pictured her tilting her head to study a line, a color, the fall of a shadow. Each imagined view of her brought warmth to his face. He could not deny the effect she had on him. It almost made him rethink his mother's commitment to his father, even after the scandal broke and shame rained down on their family.

His mother, though bowed under the dual weights of infamy and heartbreak, never denied her love for his father. It was impossible for Martin to accept at the time. He blamed his mother for her blindness to his father's deceit. Had she simply opened her eyes, she would have learned what he had been doing before the raid on his shop. If she had done so, Martin might have had some warning, some time to prepare. Instead, he had learned of his father's criminal behavior when it was printed on the front page of the *Manchester Daily Examiner and Times*.

Martin knew that this experience could have taken him one of two ways. He could have followed in his father's line, or he could run from it.

He had chosen to do everything opposite of the way his father had.

Including falling in love.

His father, as far as anyone could ever observe, adored his wife. Martin carried the fear that this tendresse was simply another of the man's frauds. Was love even real? Could Martin trust any feelings of his heart?

And did his mother, in fact, adore her husband as it had seemed? Could she truly have still loved him after his crimes came to light? Loved him, even if she could not esteem him?

But now, a new question hovered in Martin's mind. Was it possible to feel tenderly toward someone who transgressed the law, even unintentionally? When he thought of Rosanna's vast and impressive talent, he began to understand how a deceitful partner like Greystone could convince her to recreate other artists' work.

But what might she achieve by herself? He had a sudden desire to see what she could do outside the bounds of imitation. She was a woman of interesting and intelligent thoughts. Her information was fascinating, even if much of what she had told him had been in jest.

But was she involved, deeply, inextricably, in a scheme of counterfeiting and theft?

She painted the copies, that much he was confident was true. She had made no excuses for her complicity in that part of the arrangement. But the little she had said about it had not sounded like the efforts of someone making excuses to avoid punishment. In fact, she had sounded like she firmly believed she carried no blame at all.

No. She was creating unauthorized copies. For sale. Of course she was to blame.

Wasn't she?

He shook his head. This was all troublesome and fascinating and complicated. And it was secondary to the return of the stolen painting. But as much as the idea of a priceless artwork intrigued him, thoughts of Rosanna continued to intrude.

Could he find a way to liberate her from her involvement with Greystone?

Would she want to be removed from the schemes? Removed from Manchester?

Good heavens, what was he thinking? He needed to board a train immediately, or he would surely concoct a series of schemes and intrigues that would have Greystone arrested and sent to Australia, Rosanna credited with closing the case on the theft, and Martin carrying her away to London. Or Paris. Or Egypt, if that was what she wanted.

He knew nothing of her dreams and desires.

But he knew her heart.

At least the part of her heart that held him.

She might have been a forger, but no one could falsify the look she gave him when she pressed the painting into his arms. Even if she had tricked him into taking a reproduction and getting off the train so she and Greystone could go on their merry way to Liverpool and across the sea, she meant it when she kissed him. That was not a lie. He was sure of it.

And he meant it as well.

Never before had he felt for a woman the fire that Rosanna Hawkins had lit in his heart.

CHAPTER 22

ROSANNA SAT BACK DOWN, the three remaining Michelangelo reproductions on the seat before her. She stared at the work she had done with an unfamiliar combination of pride and shame.

These were excellent, flawless, perfect pictures; she knew it now that she'd seen them side by side with the original even more than she had known it before. But what was her talent beyond a way to trick and fool people?

What made the original painting so appealing? It was not the grandest of Michelangelo's works, not by anyone's estimation. It was not even particularly interesting as a composition: dozens—hundreds—of Madonna and Child pairings were both more intriguing and more intimate.

The attraction was that it was Michelangelo's. A recently rediscovered piece by the master. It was beloved because it was his. The touch of the master's brush elevated the panel.

And Rosanna had simply reproduced it. Her hand was no more useful than to fabricate facsimiles.

She stared at the three paintings until Anton pressed

himself back into the seat beside her. He never took his eyes from the group of passengers still haggling over the picture.

His chuckle held all the delight of making a profit. He rubbed his hands together as if he could already count the money. "I believe we can off-load three of these right now," he said. "I've created an absolute bidding war." He gestured with his nose toward the bargaining passengers, each eager to top the other offers in order to win the prize.

Rosanna did not remind him that she had been the one to start the conversation—he was welcome to take all the credit.

He gave a single clap. "I ought to have planned for this. Then I could have placed my man among them from the beginning and had him drive up the prices faster." He turned to Rosanna. "My bunny, are you prepared to make more money than you've dreamed?"

Her stomach clenched behind her corset. She forced what she hoped was a delighted-looking smile. "Always. What shall we do?"

He placed his arm over her shoulders. "You shall take up your paints and your brushes as soon as you can and make me another dozen of these," he said, gesturing to the paintings.

She felt him stiffen, his arm about her shoulder losing its gentle pressure.

"What is it?" she asked, almost able to keep her voice steady.

"Where is the other?" His voice was dangerous and low, that slow, familiar rumble sending waves of dread over her.

"The other what?"

He looked at her and blew out a short breath. He spoke

with his teeth clenched, each word coming out like a hiss. "The other what? Are you such a fool?" He pointed to the three paintings.

"Oh, the fourth replica?" she said, her voice containing far more air than usual. "One of your friends carried it into the group." She gestured to the haggling crowd.

"One of my—?" he began. "Ah," he said, understanding her words. "Which one?"

Would he believe her? "Large man, broad. With a hat," she said, conscious that each simple word added nothing of clarity to the picture—all of the men surrounding them could easily match that description. To add credence to her lie, she gestured vaguely to the group of people, making sure to encompass each of Anton's henchmen.

Anton stood, stumbling a bit as the train slowed for the Wigan Branch stop.

She pulled a piece of paper from her reticule and a pencil from her hair, keeping her eyes on Anton as he moved around the gathering in the aisle. She produced a quick sketch of his face, only now seeing the lines tinged with hardness, cruelty, and malice.

Rising, she tapped the nearest of the would-be customers and handed him one of the Michelangelo reproductions. "Mr. Greystone would like you to take a closer look at this to make certain you will be pleased with what you receive," she said.

The man nodded and studied the piece as though he might have any particular interest beyond owning it.

She touched the arm of one of the women at the edge of the circle; her confidence and aggressive bidding had caught Rosanna's attention. She repeated her falsehood about Anton's wish for the prospective buyers to inspect the goods, and within a few seconds, she had placed all three paintings in the hands of the passengers.

It took Anton only a moment to notice the paintings circulating through the crowd, and he attempted to regain control of the situation, barking orders to his henchmen and pleading with the assembly to hold the paintings gently as the train came to a stop in the station. Rosanna watched the growing commotion with delight.

Each person not holding a painting seemed eager to reach out and grab onto a corner. Arms stretched out; bodies angled toward each other. Tension and voices rose higher and higher. More passengers loaded onto the train, causing a logjam at the door due to the blocked aisle.

As the train's whistle signaled its impending departure, Rosanna pushed past the incoming passengers. She stepped out the rear door and onto the platform. Keeping her back to the train car was an act of will—she desperately wanted to look through the window to see if Anton had noticed her disappearance. She would know soon enough.

The Wigan Branch station was far more bustling and crowded than the last few stops had been, and Rosanna stepped into the crush of the crowd easily. It was the work of but a moment to find a uniformed officer on the platform.

But could she convince him to board the now-moving train? Could she manage to snap closed the trap she had helped to set?

"Sir," she said, waving for his attention. She pressed her sketch of Anton into his hand and made sure the officer looked at it. "This man is at this moment in that departing train car."

She pointed to the last of the passenger cars. "He is in the process of selling stolen goods. I beg you, sir, make haste."

"Ah, very good," he said, as if such messages came to him every day. "We have been warned about this one, I believe." He gave Rosanna a cursory bow and ran toward the train, leaping onto the steps as the locomotive gave a lurch along the track.

Rosanna exhaled and hurried to the station house. A crowd milled through the building, and Rosanna felt safer in the press of bodies. She made her way to the ticket agent.

"First train to Manchester, please," she said, reaching for the money in her reticule.

"Already boarding, miss," the agent said in a tired voice.

Rosanna took her ticket and hurried to the departure platform, trying not to look over her shoulder any more often than any of the other travelers. As desperate as she was to know if she was being followed, she did not want to draw any attention to herself.

She walked with purpose but without undue hurry to the middle car. As she climbed the steps of the car, she glanced over her shoulder. Nothing untoward caught her attention, and she breathed out a great sigh of relief.

Many of the seats were already taken, travelers past the halfway point from Liverpool to Manchester talking quietly to each other, sleeping, reading, or staring out the windows. Taking an empty seat in the center of the train car, she looked down at her fingers to see them shaking.

Relax, she told herself. *You have made it. You have foiled all Anton's plans, and he is likely in the hands of the authorities even now.*

She closed her eyes and let her head rest against the seat back as the train began to pull away from the station. Taking her back to Manchester. Back home. Back to Inspector Martin Harrison.

She felt a smile curve her lips as she allowed the memory of their shared moments, their kisses and glances, to steal over her. The train's movement rocked her; the murmur of the passengers blended into a hum of tranquility.

She had done it. She had stolen back the Michelangelo, turned it in to the authorities, and escaped Anton Greystone forever.

Sitting in the gently rocking train car as it gained momentum, she breathed easy for the first time all day.

This may be, she thought, *a perfect moment.*

A steely hand clamped down on her shoulder, followed by an unwelcome laugh and an oily voice dripping with insincerity. "Oh, there you are, my bunny. I almost lost you, darling."

***

For several excruciating minutes, Anton sat silently beside her, his arm over her shoulder in what must have looked like a loving gesture, but which really allowed his hand to clamp painfully around her upper arm. He let his gaze drift out the window, and she could read nothing in his expression. How did he manage to grip her so tightly and yet maintain such a casual demeanor that nobody on the train would suspect he was coercing her to stay in place?

Rosanna waited several more minutes, but when Anton still did not speak, she knew she must act. But she was no actress. Could she summon the strength to pretend just a little bit longer?

She let out a long sigh and spoke a truth. "I am glad that part has ended," she said.

She looked up at him with what she dearly hoped was a convincing gaze of adoration, an expression she had painted so many times. It was all she could manage. The look, she knew, carried pleading. But she was far from begging him to love her. She wished only for him to release her, to remove his hand from her arm and allow her to walk away.

Greystone said nothing.

Unable to muster anything approaching a smile, she felt as though she was grimacing. In fact, she was very likely grimacing; he had not loosened his grip on her arm, and pain radiated from where his fingers pressed her flesh.

"I hope those people paid a pretty sum for my—I mean, *your*—pictures."

Still he said nothing. But he looked down at her, and there was fire behind his eyes. He hummed a note that may have been an assent, his tone low and soft in a way that threatened her far more than any shouting might have. Even stilted conversation would be better than this. She felt herself slowing down and running out of words, like a music box in need of winding.

Why could she not be one of those women who keep up constant streams of chatter? Lottie would have been able to talk circles around the stiff and silent Greystone, but Rosanna had nothing left of pretense or deception. She could hardly remember to exhale. The entire enterprise was exhausting, and for what purpose? Would she even get off this train alive?

The thought staggered her. She had known that Anton was a dangerous man, but she had never before considered the possibility that her very life could be at risk.

And would that be such a loss to the world? What had she accomplished beyond the mimicry of greater talents? What had she achieved? What had she experienced?

Her mind ran circles around memories of Sunday dinners with her family, and then farther back into history to days and weeks of playful bickering with her sisters, learning decorative, feminine skills at the feet of her mother and her governesses, skills that might have enriched a life lived in drawing rooms. But what use were those skills to her now, as she sat, pinned to a train seat by a man who valued her merely as one of several avenues to wealth?

Her heart lurched thinking that she might never see her sisters again, never laugh with them, never dance in the parlor, never tease and joke about gentlemen who had caught their eyes.

Or their hearts.

Gentlemen like Martin Harrison. Oh, how had she allowed her foolish pride to overthrow her heart? How could she not have seen what he had so clearly known—that her work for Anton was deceptive? If only she had understood what Martin saw from the first, that Anton's efforts would end in dishonesty. Had she known, as easily as Martin had known, she might have severed her ties with Greystone when she had a chance.

But would she? Even had she understood Anton's ill-intent, he had fed her pride in a way that satisfied so many of her desires. Perhaps she would have continued painting for Anton, even understanding his motives were dubious, because she loved feeling important. Irreplaceable. Brilliant.

And at what cost?

Perhaps, she now recognized, at the very cost of her life.

Certainly at the cost of her heart. She felt a rush of gratitude for Martin Harrison, for the spark he ignited in her heart, for his allowing her to redeem some of her mistakes by returning the stolen Michelangelo to him.

For accepting her final kiss. She touched her fingers to her lips as though she could bring him back to her.

She swallowed and forced out a breath.

Anton glanced her way, his expression stony.

How could she have ever thought him handsome? How could she not have seen the rotten core of the man? Especially after basking in the light of Martin's regard. Martin's smile, his adoration—dare she name it love? His every look, warm with kindness and delight.

Every look except the one she could not forget. The stare he gave her when he accused her of the terrible thing that she was, as it turned out, guilty of.

Even more painful than the fear radiating from her every cell was the knowledge that Martin might never forgive her. She felt a breath shudder out of her lungs and forced herself to sit up straight, to keep the anguish hidden. She stared straight ahead.

Anton Greystone would not see her cry.

She had given him too much. Far too much. Her work and her confidence and her kisses, all of which he took as easily as though they meant nothing. She would not give him her tears.

Moving his gaze back to the window, Greystone said nothing. If they were destined to sit forever in silence, Rosanna wondering at every breath if Anton would strike, so be it. But there would not be tears.

Back stiff, lips pursed, breathing shallow, Rosanna Hawkins closed her eyes and thought of Martin. Recalled his touch, his smile. She chose to reflect on his gentleness and his goodness. She would not waste any more time contemplating any regrets. She brought to her mind a perfect image of his hand on her arm, his gentle eyes sparkling with happiness, his mouth approaching hers.

A voice floated over her shoulders. "Beg pardon, sir, but did you drop this?"

Inspector Martin Harrison stood in the aisle, holding out Anton's coat to him.

Had she conjured him? Was he real?

Anton turned and stood to face the inspector. The puzzlement that crossed Anton's face might have made Rosanna laugh in any less terrifying moment. But Inspector Harrison's face was smooth and calm. He held the topcoat that Anton had been wearing earlier in the day, the one in which Rosanna had wrapped the Michelangelo.

Anton's hands went to his waistcoat, to the very spot where Rosanna had relieved him of his pistol. Greystone's perplexity doubled, and Martin pressed a step closer, blocking Anton's egress into the aisle.

"How—? Where—?" Anton's confusion was reflected in each aborted question.

"Is it yours, sir?" the inspector pressed, giving the coat a small shake.

Anton nodded and regained his composure. With his signature ingratiating smile, he said, "It is, indeed, and I thank you for its safe return."

Rosanna could practically see the thoughts whirring in Anton's mind. When and how had he lost his coat? Had he carried it onto the eastbound train? Had he held it, or even worn it as he made his way through the cars to Rosanna?

If more questions occurred to him, there was no time for him to ask them. As Anton reached for the coat, Martin grasped both of Anton's wrists and shackled them with locking cuffs.

The look of surprise on Anton's face thrilled Rosanna.

Martin seemed to stand a bit taller. "I am Inspector Martin Harrison."

Rosanna felt a flutter of pride at those words.

Martin continued to speak. "I am not sure how I should address you, sir, since your pockets held cards in a variety of names, but I assure you, whatever you are called, you are hereby under arrest for theft, possession of stolen goods, and conspiracy to sell stolen property. You may consider holding your commentary until you have called a solicitor, sir."

Anton yanked at his shackles, but Martin held him fast.

With a shake of his head, Martin said, "I am confident you would not wish to look a fool to Miss Hawkins. Nor in front of some of England's finest officers."

Martin gestured around the train car, and Rosanna noticed several uniformed officers standing from their seats and approaching from discreet distances. She began to laugh in relief.

Oh, dear.

Both men cast their eyes on her, Greystone with a scathing sneer, Martin with something that looked like reproach. She looked directly into his face and said, "Inspector, I am sorry."

With none of the warmth she hoped to hear from him, the inspector said, "I have not finished with you, Miss Hawkins."

He released Anton Greystone to the hands of two officers and nodded them out the connecting door and away.

CHAPTER 23

INDEED, HE HAD not finished with her.

He hoped he would not finish with Rosanna Hawkins for quite some time. Perhaps never. But for now, other police business would keep him occupied. To Martin's great relief, Greystone's guards, two of the railway's security officers, kept the thief far away from Rosanna.

Martin removed a notebook from his pocket and made a careful accounting of all that had occurred since he'd boarded this train. He did not want to mistake any of the events, as he would surely be called upon to testify about each of them.

They rode back to Manchester Victoria station in silence, disembarking in the company of several other officers. As they stepped down from the railcar, Martin saw the two security officers, one on either side of Anton Greystone, resolutely ignoring his wheedling complaints.

Martin, looking down at Miss Hawkins, said, "One more moment, please. Stay beside me."

Joining the officers, he placed one hand on the arm of the

shackled prisoner while the other remained on the canvas bag slung over his own shoulder.

He kept his eyes, however, on Miss Hawkins as he placed himself between the prisoner and the lady.

She breathed in short hitches, and he wondered if she was crying.

He wondered, with a combination of the professional neutrality of an officer and the genuine affection of a potential suitor, what she was feeling just now. Guilt? Or was it fear? Relief? Despair? Or something else altogether? Horror at the recognition that her employer was as unworthy of her trust as Martin's own father had been unworthy of his?

She said nothing at all.

Whatever she might be feeling, he would not repeat the mistake of letting her out of his view. She had made too many escapes in the past few hours for him to trust her entirely. He would keep her nearby. For police purposes, of course. Of course.

Collier and Wiggins stood with another small knot of officers at the station platform. Martin felt a sigh of relief escape him. He could not wait to turn this prisoner over to Collier.

The relief came as a surprise. Should he not desire to see this through to the very end? Ought he wish to walk Greystone to the prison house himself, slam the door, and turn the key?

Here he was, handing over a prolific and dangerous criminal so another officer could complete the investigation, wrap up the case, and very likely take the credit for the arrest. And Martin did not care in the least. The only part of this case that held any further interest to him was Miss Hawkins.

Rosanna.

Without any fuss, Martin saw Greystone passed into Collier's custody.

The other officer proceeded to march Greystone away, making up for Martin's silence with a ceaseless stream of official chatter that promised to be only the beginning of the prisoner's punishments.

Martin handed the canvas bag to Wiggins and said in a low voice, "This ought to be returned to the exhibition at once. I believe others will follow."

"Indeed," Wiggins said. "We have men at the Liverpool station prepared to look into any unclaimed baggage from the train."

"Which they will treat with the utmost care, of course," Martin said for Rosanna's benefit.

Leading Rosanna away from the still-crowded station platform, Martin was pleased that she still held on to his arm. Their silence had continued too long, and he spoke as they walked.

"Miss Hawkins, I believe you were uninformed of the scope of Greystone's schemes and therefore innocent," Martin said, "but I cannot pretend you have no fault here."

Rosanna's eyes, which had been turned toward Martin with a lovely, hopeful expression, filled now with tears.

"I know," she said, her voice hitching. "My fault is in my pride and my desire to impress, but please, Inspector, please believe that I have not intentionally committed any crime." She looked up into his face, a flush suffusing her cheeks. "I know you're unable to forgive my unwitting connection to that man's crimes," she said, gesturing toward the retreating group, "any more than you can forgive the father who took your childhood innocence from you." She breathed in as though speaking the words took a physical toll, and a shine gathered in her eyes. "I do not deserve special treatment, but I beg you to find a way to forgive my ignorance and my gullibility."

These final words came out in a shudder as her tears broke and she began to cry. "Please ignore this display," she said, attempting to cover her mouth and eyes with one hand. "I have had quite a trying day."

He did not wish to make her cry, so he hurried to speak.

"You misunderstand." He shook his head and placed himself before her so she might more easily look at him if she chose to do so. "I cannot justify my father's crimes, but I can forgive the man. It will take me some time to do so fully as he hurt my mother terribly, and I have never once heard him ask for any manner of forgiveness." He tilted his head closer to hers, and he caught her fleeting glance. "Should he do so, my efforts would redouble, I assure you."

She took a breath and finally looked up into his face. "Then perhaps someday you could forgive my foolishness?"

The pain in her words made his heart ache. Had he made the situation that much worse for her?

"There is no need for you to seek forgiveness from me for being taken in by Mr. Greystone," he said. He saw her flinch at the sound of the name. "And if you prefer, we shall not speak of him again."

She nodded in apparent relief.

"But that is not the end of this," he said, his voice still

soft, but firm. "You have stolen something as well, Miss Hawkins." He held her in a serious gaze.

New tears spilled from her eyes as she shook her head in denial.

"It was not me," she whispered. "All the stolen pieces should be found by the Liverpool police, and all will be as it was."

Now it was Martin's turn to shake his head. "I'm afraid nothing will ever be as it was." Seeing the anxiety in Rosanna's face, he reached for both her hands. "You have stolen my heart, and I shall never be the same."

Her lips twisted in a moment of confusion. Her breath hitched. She shook her head. "I cannot know how to believe you. I was so certain that you must despise me."

Ducking his head nearer to hers, he said, "Never. I do and will and shall adore you forever."

"Can it be true?" She looked caught between a sob and a smile.

He could hardly leave her in doubt, and he could think of only one way to make her believe him.

Martin raised his hand to her lovely cheek, erasing the line of a tear before he leaned in and kissed Rosanna's mouth. His hand slid beneath the glorious knot of her hair as he pulled her gently closer. He felt her laugh against his lips. His arms moved around her back, and he took in every element of their connection—each place her skin met his, every scent and whisper of wind. Everything she had shown him about art was now in play as he truly noticed what he was feeling.

Might every kiss, might every moment be so full of

wonder, now that she had taught him to truly comprehend what he saw?

As she pulled away, she held his face close and, with another delighted laugh, whispered, "Ought you to be seen kissing an accomplice to a major theft, Inspector?"

He drew back. "Is that what you are, now?" He did not even pretend to hide his smile.

She moved her hands to the front of his vest. "Perhaps you would reform me, sir."

"It would certainly be worth the effort to try," he answered, and their smiles were soon concealed in another kiss.

MANCHESTER HERALD-TRIBUNE

October 21, 1857

Farewell to Summer's Treasures
Lottie Hawkins

As the summer wanes and autumn shows her colors, the artistic experience of a lifetime for so many Mancunians comes to an end. Those of us who frequented the Art Treasures Exhibition this summer have watched with both fascination and sadness as the masterworks have been boxed and removed, the glass walls have come down, and the field itself has begun to regrow.

Was this exhibition only the beginning for Manchester? Will we soon have increasing and more permanent opportunities to experience cultural events? This reporter hopes that the excitement of the previous months, including royal visits, keeps the flame of art appreciation alive for years to come.

In addition to overseeing the safety of the exhibition, our very own Manchester constabulary has proven itself notable for thwarting an attempt at thievery. Sources close to the police force suggest that the Peelers did not let a moment pass between an attempted heist and a successful return of priceless paintings. As further information is available, count on finding the full story here in the *Herald-Tribune*. Rest assured that we are safe under the watch of our perceptive and discerning police force.

If such adventure is beyond your curiosity, fear not. Further interest in paintings, sculptures, drawings, and other artworks can be satisfied by seeking admittance to one or another of Manchester's fine families' salons, where collectors are eager to keep conversations about art free-flowing.

CHAPTER 24

Manchester, April 1858

ROSANNA ADJUSTED THE painting a fraction of an inch on its display easel. Although she was certain the angle was not likely to be noticed by anyone but herself, she desired to control what she could.

There was no way to control the coming reaction to the painting, though. Neither this one nor any of the others.

After each of the stolen masterpieces had been silently returned to the walls and the exhibition finished its course, Rosanna continued to walk past the venue, watching the building come down, dismantled piece by piece. When nothing remained but the parkland, she had spent the winter months at work before her easels, painting not for Greystone but for herself. Not imitations of masterworks; rather, whatever struck her fancy.

And her fancy unfurled in delight.

For the first time since Rosanna had been under the tutelage of her governess and her painting masters, she felt free to paint the way she had always desired to. And she went home to her parents' Cheetham Hill manor to do it. After the excitement of the summer, she took comfort in the routine of her youth.

She sat on the floor in the corner of the morning room and painted the way the light moved across the gilded picture frames.

She sat in a small parlor with Lottie and watched how the candlelight burnished creamy paper. She attempted to capture the glint of a flame's glow against her sister's hand, her inkpot, and her pen as Lottie scribbled away, page after page, writing news items as well as stories of her own invention.

Rosanna spent hours and hours in the music room, watching Ella as she moved from piano to violin, capturing the sway of her hips and shoulders as Ella became immersed in her music. Rosanna dabbed paint in patterns that suggested not only what she could see but what she heard and how the music felt.

She painted her mother, seated near a window as she worked her tiny, careful stitches in linen, as true in her reproduction of each thread as she was to the halo effect of the light on her mother's hair. She followed her into the garden and the greenhouse, painting the images of plants and flowers, the feeling of color and light and growth.

She painted and repainted a study of Queen Victoria, bent in intimate whisper with her daughter, the background blurred into a wash of color and shadow, perfectly reminiscent to Rosanna of the gallery, but subtly universal in its texture. It could be a painting of any mother and child in any room.

And today, her mother's salon would hold the best of the

new work she had done. Rosanna understood that many of her mother's guests would be alarmed at the paintings. They would find her exploration and invention with color and light disturbing, particularly those guests who had paid Anton Greystone for the privilege of owning Rosanna's Renaissance reproductions, paintings that represented all things approved and acceptable.

She understood as well that each mode of now-common art had been met with resistance at the time of its own conception. She imagined patrons of the arts all through history gasping and shaking their heads, either hiding or revealing their dismay as each new mode, from cave painting to representative portraiture to images of the Divine, made their debuts.

Not that Rosanna had any notion of founding a new style of painting. She did not expect other painters to turn away from the expressive realism of the day and begin to paint what they *felt* rather than what they *saw*. She simply took joy—deep, significant joy—in creating something that came from within her creative mind. The mind she was learning to trust for the first time.

Rosanna knew she could likely earn a handsome living by continuing to produce art after the manner of the masters, even if she could no longer bring herself to make exact copies. Her taste for flawless reproduction had never returned after Anton's arrest.

New ideas, forms, and explorations awaited her oils and brushes.

Not to mention her heart.

At that thought, Rosanna heard a throat clear behind her.

She turned to see Martin Harrison, resplendent in his plaid waistcoat, his hair curling fashionably over his pristine white collar.

She gestured to the room, filled tastefully with her paintings and her mother's flowers.

"Well?" she asked, smiling warmly into his face.

"I shall give you my honest impressions in a moment," he said. "But before I can attend to the art, I must gaze upon the artist."

Rosanna laughed, delighted with Martin's teasing tone. She curtsied and took a turn about him, never taking her eyes from his adoring face.

He considered her with an air of serious study, glancing from the top of her hair to the shoes that peeked out from beneath her remarkably full skirt. "Something seems to be missing." He made a spinning motion with his finger, and she turned before him, worried she had somehow bumped into wet paint and spoiled her gown.

"Ah," he said, a smile of triumph on his face. "I have it." He reached into his vest and withdrew an item which he then tucked into the curls gathered at the back of her head.

"What—?" she began, but then felt her hair and laughed. He had slipped a paintbrush, slim and delicate, into the bounty of her hair.

"Now you look like the artist I love," he said, placing a kiss upon her cheek.

Even after all these months, Rosanna never failed to feel a trembling of delight at his touch, his smiles, and his kisses. She reached for his hand to take him through the room.

"Wait," he said softly. "I have something else for you."

Her cheeks flushed as he reached into his jacket pocket. *Would he propose?* she wondered. It would make today perfect.

But he handed her an envelope. "I do hope you don't mind, but since it was delivered to my address, I opened it."

Opening the heavy paper envelope, she slipped out a folded sheet of stationery with an ornate crest emblazoned upon it. Unfolding the note, she read.

> *Dearest Miss Hawkins,*
>
> *I owe you a sincere and heartfelt thanks for your assistance in the recovery of some truly priceless artworks. But at the risk of sounding selfish and uncultured, my deeper thanks must be for the original portrait you sent of me and my daughter. I have rarely seen a painting of myself that I like, and never before one that captures my attention so thoroughly. Your style is daring, yet I feel myself recalling the delight of our visit to Manchester that day every time I look at it. You have captured the essence of our experience, and I thank you sincerely for the gift.*
>
> *Should you feel inclined to visit, I and my family would love to sit for a more formal painting with you at any time.*
>
> *Please accept my very best wishes for your continued success,*
>
> *Victoria*

Rosanna stared, open-mouthed, at the words on the paper. She leaned closer to Martin and whispered, "*Victoria?* Just like that? As though we are dear friends?"

Martin grinned. "You are positively aglow. I assume this means I am forgiven for sending her one of your paintings without your permission."

Rosanna smiled in wonder. "I did not notice any of the studies missing. Which painting did you send her?"

"The truest of them," Martin replied.

She understood completely.

So overwhelmed did she feel, she could not even jest with him. "I believe you are forgiven."

"And for telling her the story of your daring?"

Rosanna turned the card over, as if searching for more writing. When nothing else appeared, she laid her finger along the side of her nose.

With a wink, she said, "She did seem to forget to offer me a knighthood. Perhaps in the next letter."

Martin gazed at her, looking as delighted for her good fortune as she could feel herself.

"Not that I have finished admiring you, but I should love to be shown the paintings now," he said, taking her hand and tucking it into the crook of his arm.

She guided him through the room, stopping here and there to tell a silly, pretend story about one of the paintings. She found delight in his reactions to her games. He had found the confidence that allowed him to laugh with her, and she adored him for it.

He pointed out a painting he'd not seen before. "And this one?"

"This, as you can see, is a bouquet of my mother's loveliest summer blooms. Notice how the light sparkles from the drops of morning dew, signifying that the bunch has been picked only now." She looked at him, loving the way he studied her painting. "These flowers are for a very important event," she went on, attempting to keep her voice airy and playful. "For this July day, a lady will carry these flowers down the chapel aisle to meet her beloved at the altar."

"Wedding flowers?" Martin said, still studying the painting.

"Not just any wedding flowers," Rosanna said, a catch in her voice. "You can see, if you look closely, that this is a very special bouquet, filled with only the best colors. The colors that promise a life filled with love." She gestured to the blooms in the painting as she spoke, hoping to keep her voice from trembling. "Colors of happiness and joy. The colors I see when I am with you."

"And who," he asked, turning to face her fully, "is the fortunate bride, whose flowers are only of the very best colors?"

"She is me," Rosanna said simply.

He looked at the painting, nodded, and looked back at Rosanna.

"But there is a small problem," Martin said, unable to hide his smile. "You are not, as far as I know, engaged."

She shook her head. "Not yet. But I believe someone shall ask me soon." Her smile matched his own.

"Is that so?" he asked, taking both her hands in his and pressing them to his chest.

She nodded, delight coursing through her.

"And if someone asked," he said, his warm eyes never leaving hers, "would you accept his proposal? If he were a man of integrity and good standing, perhaps one recently promoted within the ranks of the Manchester constabulary?"

"Only if he is the man who holds my hands and my heart," she whispered, pressing her fingers more firmly against his.

He seemed to be memorizing her face.

With the smallest shake of his head, he said, "You have so much to offer the world. Nothing must be allowed to diminish your ability to paint. I should hate to create any boundaries that might get in the way."

"It is because of you," she said, "that I can do my work. Daily you renew my confidence." She hoped he could see how much she meant the words.

He seemed to breathe her in, absorbing the moment, the surroundings, the feelings of the afternoon. "Are you willing to be both an artist and a wife? Will you," he said, his own voice lowering to a near-whisper, "do me the honor of creating a life with me?"

Rosanna was surprised to feel tears collecting in her eyes. Hardly trusting her voice, she nodded, and Martin released one hand to wipe a fallen tear from her cheek. He wrapped his arm about her, and, without breaking their embrace, they turned to face her paintings.

"Someone in history may have once been this happy," she said.

"As I understand it," he murmured into her hair, "many have felt so."

She grinned at him. "Perhaps there were others who thought they were in love," she said. "But I shall spend the rest of our lives showing the world what love looks like." She gestured to the room filled with her paintings.

He turned her to face him again. "Truly? And what," he asked, tucking a curl behind her ear, "does love look like?"

"Close your eyes," she whispered, rising upon her toes and drawing his face toward her own, "and I'll show you."

ACKNOWLEDGMENTS

ONCE UPON A TIME, my mom walked into our elementary school and told the nuns in charge that she'd like to teach the students about paintings. Not how to paint, but how to understand and recognize some of the masters. What followed was an introduction to art that, for the kids in our small Midwestern town far from a gallery or museum, gave a glimpse of history and possibility, all at the hands of a true lover of art.

She planted that same appreciation deep inside me, and I'm so grateful for a basic understanding and recognition of beautiful things that has stayed with me for many years.

And so, those who can't *do*, write novels.

I'm so grateful for both reader friends and writer friends who fill in the gaps, whether they be in confidence, in story, in knowledge of guns and trains, or in motivation. This job is an unexaggerated million times better because of you.

With gratitude for at least pretending to be interested, I thank my high school creative writing classes, who watched the process, responded to revisions, applauded on command,

and encouraged more kissing (in the story, I mean). I loved teaching you people.

Many thanks to the Proper Romance team, including Lisa Mangum, Heidi Gordon, Chris Schoebinger, Callie Hansen, and Haley Haskins. Thanks to Heather Ward for the cover and Breanna Anderl for typesetting the book. I love being part of this community. Thank you all for bringing my stories to life.

And of course, thank you to each of you who loves my books. Without you, I'm just talking to myself, which everyone knows leads nowhere pleasant. Thank you for making this effort into a conversation.

DISCUSSION
QUESTIONS

1. The Art Treasures Exhibition was a real event. The building was constructed in the summer of 1857 in a field outside the city of Manchester, and it actually held more artworks than the Louvre Museum in Paris. Is there a historical event that you'd love to experience? Where? When?

2. The middle 1850s saw a surge in popularity of men's beards. For soldiers fighting in the Crimean, beards were a necessity. Not only were razors hard to come by but the facial hair helped to keep the soldiers warm. As a result, a common assumption in England was that bearded men were brave war heroes. Anton Greystone took advantage of that assumption to earn the trust of his buyers. Is there a "look" that convinces you someone is trustworthy? Or is there a style that turns you away?

3. Martin's work as a police officer is sometimes referred to as "Bobby" or "Peeler." Both those names derive from a two-time prime minister, Robert Peel, who is considered the father of modern policing. Is there an occupation or

career that you know of that takes its nickname from a founder or originator?

4. Do you have a favorite work of art? Have you seen it in person? Does the artwork feel different when you're standing in front of it?

5. Rosanna goes into something of a trance when she's working. Is there an activity you do that takes you into "the zone" and away from reality?

6. Creating art takes talent and courage. Is copying an existing work still art? How about coloring? Crafting? Do you consider *your* art to be art? Why or why not?

7. Sometimes we follow in our parents' footsteps. But sometimes, like Martin Harrison, we run fast in the other direction. What traits of your parents do you continue? Which do you choose to leave behind?

8. Many (if not most) new styles of art—whether painting, clothing design, music composition, architecture, or sculpture, to name a few—are shocking to their first audiences. Rosanna's painting master was disgusted by her "muddy wallpaper" (a phrase I stole from an early critic of Impressionism). Do you have a favorite artistic period? Do you know how the art of that period was received when it was new?

9. Martin and Rosanna have a moment—several long moments—when they lock gazes and stare into each other's eyes. Research suggests this is a fast-forward button to intimacy. Are you comfortable with prolonged eye contact? Have you ever tried the long stare with someone? How did it make you feel?

10. The paintings named in the book actually hung in the

Art Treasures Exhibition, including the unfinished *Manchester Madonna* by Michelangelo. Do you agree with Martin that such a piece is hardly worth notice? Or does the touch of the master's brush make anything, even a sketch, priceless?

ABOUT THE AUTHOR

Photo by Scott Wilhite

By night, Rebecca Anderson writes historical romances. By day, she sets aside her pseudonym and resumes her life as Becca Wilhite, who loves hiking, Broadway shows, rainstorms, food, books, and movies. She lives in the mountains and adores the ocean. She dreams of travel but loves staying home. Happiness is dabbling in lots of creative activities, afternoon naps, and cheese. All the cheese.

You can find her online at beccawilhite.com.

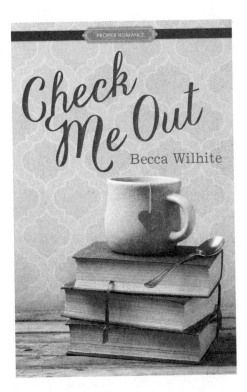